The Legend

A Novel by Perry D. Jones

Synergy Books

Prologue — *"I Need Love"* (Intro)

"When I'm alone in my room, sometimes I stare at the wall..." — LL Cool J

It's quiet.

Not the peaceful kind. Not the kind that settles into your chest and rocks you to sleep.

This is the kind of quiet that asks questions you usually run from.

I'm sitting on the edge of the bed, not fully dressed, not fully ready to move. Alexis is still asleep behind me—one arm stretched across my side of the bed like a gentle reminder.

Her love doesn't ask for performance. It just shows up. Consistent. Solid. Soft in ways I didn't know I needed.

But I'm still learning how to let it in.

There's a notebook on the nightstand.
One of my rhymebooks.

I've started filling pages again—nothing fancy, just lines. Feelings. Fragments. A bar here and there. Something Darius used to say. Something I overheard from Rodney. A memory Simone brought up without realizing it cracked something open in me.

I write because talking doesn't always cut it. Because some days, what I feel doesn't have punctuation yet.

I know this much now:
I need love.

Alexis's love—because she's teaching me that safety doesn't mean silence.
Simone's love—because she sees me clearer than I ever expected, and loves me anyway.
Rodney's love—because it's an extension of the bond I lost, and a reminder that I still have something to give.
And maybe most importantly… I need my own.

I've spent so many years running from that.

Hiding in work.
In guilt.
In purpose.

But I can't map anything forward without loving the man holding the pen.

The Map helped me find the path.
Now I have to learn how to walk it—*with my whole self in the room.*

Even the broken pieces.

Even the quiet.

Even the love.

Chapter 1: "Sweet You" — Phonte

"Some say it was a blessing in disguise / Scratch that, girl you are a lesson from the skies."

Alexis made breakfast again.

Nothing fancy—just eggs, wheat toast, and those little chicken sausages she says she only buys when she's trying to "love herself better." She moved around my kitchen like she's been here longer than she actually has, humming something soft that wasn't on the radio but sounded like home anyway.

She was wearing one of my old t-shirts.

Big on her. Faded black cotton with a cracked "Tribe Called Quest" logo across the chest. It used to be my go-to sleep shirt back when I was trying to hold memories together with fabric. Now it's hers, and seeing her in it felt like something sacred.

Old school intimacy.
Like mixtapes.
Like handwritten notes.
Like love that doesn't need to shout to be real.

She caught me looking at her while she flipped the eggs.

"What?" she said, not even turning all the way around.

"Nothing," I said.

She glanced back at me over her shoulder. "You keep looking at me like you're trying to figure out if this is real."

I didn't respond. Mostly because she wasn't wrong.

Some days, it still feels like I'm waiting for the catch. The fallout. The moment she remembers I'm not the cleanest, smoothest version of myself. That I come with history, hesitation, and a tendency to overthink love like it's a riddle.

But she never treats me like a project.
She treats me like a place.
Like something worth coming back to.

"Why you looking at your phone like it offended you?" she asked, setting a mug in front of me like she'd clocked my thoughts.

"Because I'm trying to write a text I'm not gonna send," I admitted.

"Oh, so you're in one of those moods."

She smiled. I laughed. And just like that, we were good again. That's the thing about Alexis—she gets me. Not in a big, dramatic, rom-com monologue kind of way. Just... in the quiet. The in-between. She doesn't reach to fix me. She just *shows up*. And these days, that's starting to feel like more than enough.

She reached across the table and grabbed my hand like she was saying, *I see you.*
And I believed her.

Some say it was a blessing in disguise.
Scratch that—*girl, you are a lesson from the skies.*

After we ate, she curled up on the couch and tucked her legs underneath her. Still wearing the shirt. Still humming something low and jazzy. I watched her from the kitchen for a second—wanted to say something about how she makes this space feel like more than just a house.

But I didn't.

I just stood there, appreciating the stillness.
That's new for me too.

Later, I'm driving to The Spot. No music. Just the sound of the engine and the slow hum of my own thoughts.

Rodney is supposed to meet me there. He wants to talk about an idea—some kind of event, something big. Lately, he's been stepping into his voice more, and I won't lie... it makes me feel something.

Pride. Fear. Joy. All tangled up like old headphone cords.

Sometimes when I look at him, I see Darius. Not just in the face, but in the way he moves. That quiet fire. That weight he carries and tries to pretend he doesn't. And some days, he looks at me like... like I'm supposed to have answers I don't even have for myself yet.

I park the car and sit for a second, staring at the building. It's changed. It's growing. And so am I.

But I still hear Darius in my head sometimes.

"You don't gotta earn love, bro. You just gotta let it in."

I'm trying.

Every day, I'm trying.

Alexis texted me while I was parked.
Just a little heart and a "Have a good one, love."

I stared at that word for a while.

Love.

I used to say it like it was borrowed.
Now, I'm starting to say it like it's mine.

I walk into The Spot and find Rodney already there—
hoodie up, head bobbing to something in his
headphones. He doesn't look up right away, which
gives me a moment to just… watch him.

He's taller now. Sharper. Carrying himself different.
There's still a weight on him, yeah, but there's also
light. And I don't know when it happened, but this
kid—this young man—is starting to feel like my own.

It scares me a little.

But maybe that's how I know it's real.

Chapter 2: "Picture Perfect" — Eric Roberson

"Girl, you are picture perfect…"

She would've liked Alexis.

I mean, really liked her.

Mama had a way of looking at somebody and seeing past the whole surface show. She didn't need a full conversation to know who you were. A nod, a word, a breath—you were already clocked. And if she ever told you, *"Mmm. That one good,"* you could rest easy. That was Mariama Patterson's stamp. Final and full.

Alexis got that kind of approval from me without ever meeting her.
And that morning—watching her move around my space like she belonged there, wearing my old Tribe shirt like it was always hers, humming something soft and spiritual in the background?

Yeah.
I wished Mama could've seen her like that.

Now I'm at The Spot, and the morning is still with me.

The building is mostly quiet, early sun pouring through the windows just right. The kind of light that makes you feel like you're supposed to *notice something*. Appreciate it. I'm standing by the mural near the main office, staring at the colors we picked for the community wall. Deep reds, soft oranges, shades of peace and legacy.

Rodney's supposed to meet me later.

But right now, it's just me.
And Mama.
In memory, in rhythm.

My mother's name was Mariama.
Gullah born. Strong-boned. Soft-spoken until she didn't feel like being.

She had this way of turning a regular sentence into scripture.
You'd walk away thinking you just had a normal conversation, and days later it would hit you—*that woman just rewrote your whole outlook in eight words or less.*

She used to say, *"Ev'ry time ya heart too full, let it breathe lil bit, or it'll bust."*

She'd tell me that when I was younger—when I'd come in the house frustrated or overwhelmed, stuffing everything down like feelings were bricks I had to carry without complaint.

And today? I heard it again.

Not from her lips.
But in the way Alexis had reached across the table this
morning and just held my hand.

She didn't ask me to unpack anything.
She just made space for me to breathe.

That's the kind of love Mama wanted for me. I know
it.
And not just the romantic kind.

She wanted me to have *safe* love.
Whole love.
The kind that wraps itself around you without
tightening like a grip.

I leaned against the wall and looked up at the high
windows. Dust danced in the light like something
sacred. I remembered Mama in the garden, her scarf
tied loose at the back, her voice carrying low as she
talked to the collards like they needed to hear her
speak softness to grow.

She believed things bloomed when spoken to kindly.

She believed people did, too.

I wonder what she would say to me now.
Watching me try to step into this life like I'm not still
worried it'll all vanish if I blink wrong.

She'd probably smile that half-smile she used to give
when she knew I was thinking too hard.

Probably say, *"Malik, baby... love ain't no puzzle. Stop
trying to solve it. Just hold it 'til it fit in your hands right."*

And maybe I'd listen this time.

Maybe.

My phone buzzed. Alexis again. Another heart. No
words.

She was still in my house. Still wearing that shirt. Still
humming songs into spaces I'd been trying to fill for
years.

And I thought again:

She's not just someone I love.

She's someone I wish my mother could've met.

Chapter 3: "On The Way" — Little Brother

"Now we on the way y'all, we on the way y'all / The shinin light lookin for a better day y'all / We on the way y'all, we on the way y'all / We makin moves, ain't there no time to play y'all."

Rodney was already mid-conversation when I walked into the common room.

His hoodie was half-off, headphones hanging around his neck like they'd been there all night. A couple of the younger kids had surrounded him, all of them locked into some animated discussion about sneakers, music, and who had the best album rollout this decade.

He looked like Darius in that moment.

Not the face, exactly—but the calm.
That still-center energy. Like he didn't have to raise his voice to lead.
People just leaned in.

And I felt it in my chest.

That shift.
The quiet kind.

The one where you realize this isn't just a kid you're mentoring anymore.

This is somebody looking at you like *you matter.*

"Yo, Mr. Malik," he called out, breaking away from the circle.
I nodded and walked over, offering him one of those half-handshake, half-embrace things we've settled into. Not too formal. Not too familiar. But real.

"You got a sec?" he asked. "Wanna run something by you."

I nodded. "Yeah, what's up?"

He looked over his shoulder, lowered his voice. "Not here. Just... when you got a minute."

That tone. That pause. It carried weight.
It wasn't just an idea. It was something *personal.*
Something real.

We walked the perimeter of The Spot—past the murals, the quiet classrooms, the corner where a few donated keyboards sat waiting for new music. He didn't say much at first, just shoved his hands deep into his hoodie pockets and took slow, deliberate steps like the ground was telling him something.

I didn't rush him.

Darius used to walk like that when he was sitting with something.
Didn't matter what it was—grief, joy, a wild idea—he needed the rhythm of movement to help untangle it.

Rodney moved the same way.

And I was learning to be patient with it.

He finally spoke as we rounded the back of the building.

"You ever think about how many people just... don't know what this place is?" he asked. "Like, they don't even know what happens in here."

"All the time," I said. "Been trying to fix that for years."

Rodney nodded. "I got an idea. It's not all the way figured out yet, but it could be dope."

I let the silence hang.

He kept talking.

"We bring in music, spoken word, dance, art—like everything. Get folks who been here, who *believe* in this place, to show what it's meant to them. But not like a talent show. More like a... like a cultural thing. Like celebration *and* blueprint."

He looked up at me, eyes focused now. "And not just the kids that are still here. Like, the ones who came through and *made it*. The ones in college now, or starting businesses, or mentoring. They could tell their stories. Perform if they want. Just... let people *see the success*, not just the structure."

That hit me.

Because I knew those stories.
I remembered the first kid who cried in my office after getting their first job.
The girl who showed me her scholarship letter with her hands shaking.
The boy who came back from basic training and said, *"Mr. Malik, you saved me."*

I remembered all of them.

But I'd never thought to *show* them.

I looked at Rodney again.

He wasn't pitching.
He was claiming something.
Ownership. Vision. Forward motion.

And the truth?

It scared me. Just a little.

Not because I didn't believe in him.
But because I could feel what was happening.

That **father-son shift**.
That space between "let me guide you" and "I trust
your lead."

"You serious about this?" I asked.

Rodney nodded. "Yeah. I want it to be something
real."

We stood there in the quiet.

"You want it to be real?" I said. "Then let's make it
real."

He smiled—wide this time, like he wasn't sure
whether to dap me or hug me.

So he did both.

We walked back to the front entrance—quicker now,
full of the kind of momentum you can't force.

And as we stepped inside, the hallway glowing with late-afternoon light, I heard it faintly in my head. Not a voice, not music. Just... a rhythm.

Now we on the way y'all, we on the way y'all...

And yeah. We really were.

Back in my office, while Rodney peeled off toward the rec room to catch up with a few others, I sat down, unlocked my phone, and opened a new message.

To: Alexis
This kid. He's got vision. Got heart, too. Makes you proud without even trying.

I hovered over the send button for a second.

Deleted the "you'd be proud of him too" part I almost typed.
It felt like too much.
Too revealing.

But I sent the message anyway.

Her reply came back thirty seconds later.

Two emojis. That was it.

Black heart. Crown.

She got it. She always did.

The crown wasn't just for Rodney.
It was for the moment.
For the legacy.
For the quiet feeling I couldn't quite name yet but
was starting to understand.

Chapter 4: "Afro Blue" — Robert Glasper

"Dream of a land my soul is from…"

The building was quiet again.

Rodney had gone home. The kids were long gone. The fluorescent lights overhead buzzed like they always did when the air got still. I didn't turn on any music—just sat at the piano in the back room and let my hands find the keys.

I don't play like a professional.
Just enough to let my thoughts breathe.

Sometimes the chords don't land quite right.
But the rhythm always does.

Today felt like movement.

Not the kind you chase, but the kind that *finds you.* That conversation with Rodney cracked something open in me. A door I didn't even know I'd kept shut. One minute we're walking the perimeter of the building, and the next, I'm thinking about college fairs and cultural showcases and booking flights for alumni I haven't seen in a decade.

He doesn't even realize it yet, but he lit a fire.

And I felt it sitting under my ribs all day.

I kept playing soft chords. Nothing structured. Just tones and memory.

And then the melody of "Afro Blue" started to float up from my fingertips. Not perfectly. Not precisely. But honest.

That's all I had in me tonight—*honesty in pieces.*

Dream of a land my soul is from...

That line echoed in my head, even though no one was singing it.
The piano spoke it.
The air around me held it.

And I knew what it meant.

This place—The Spot.
These kids.
Rodney.
Even this old piano with the slightly chipped middle C...

They were all part of a place I came from, even if I didn't grow up in it.

I looked around the room.

Felt the stillness shift just a little.

The Spot had always been more than just a center. It was *a place for breathing*. For releasing. For building. But even as that thought settled into me, something tugged at the edge of it.

Money.

Not loud. Not urgent. Not yet.
But present.

I'd been juggling grants. Chasing donations. Making calls that led to callbacks that led to promises that led to... nothing.

Rodney's vision was beautiful. Powerful. Necessary.

But part of me knew—we couldn't build off vision alone.

Still, I stayed with the music.

Because if I let the weight of that part take over too soon, I'd never move at all.

I opened my journal.

The same one I've been writing in since before The Spot had real walls.

Wrote:

Rodney's idea is brilliant.
Scares me.
Because I see Darius in him.
But I also see me.
Not the man I was—
the one I'm still becoming.
What if I actually belong in this part of his story?

I paused.

Then added:

Legacy is never one person.
It's a rhythm we keep handing back and forth.

I thought of Mama.

She would've loved today.
Not just the moment—but the motion.

She'd have smiled at Rodney, told him his spirit was older than his body.
She always said that about me, too.

"Ya carryin' more than ya age, Malik. Just make sure it don't carry you."

I closed the journal.

Kept playing.

Let the music hold what my words couldn't.

And somewhere between the A minor and the soft
lift of the pedal,
I stopped thinking about what I needed to do next.

I just let myself be here.
In this note.
In this breath.
In this quiet.

Afro Blue filled the room.
No lyrics.
Just truth.

Interlude: "The Call"

The music had stopped, but I wasn't ready to move yet.
The room was still humming in its own way, like it knew I needed to sit in it just a little longer.

That's when my phone rang.

Simone.

Not a text.
Not a missed call from earlier.
A real call.

I answered without clearing my throat.

"Hey, baby."

"Hey, Daddy."
Soft. Familiar. The sound of her voice always made me stand up a little straighter.

"You good?" I asked.

"I'm alright. Just wanted to check in. Haven't heard from you in a couple days, and that usually means you're avoiding something."

I laughed. "Wow. That's how we opening this?"

"I'm just saying."

Her tone was playful, but I knew her well enough to hear the layers underneath. She wasn't calling just to mess with me. She was reaching out to make sure I hadn't disappeared into my own head again.

"I've been... thinking," I said.

"Dangerous," she replied.

I smiled. "About The Spot. About... this kid I've been working with. He's got ideas. Big ones. Got me thinking about where all this is going."

She was quiet for a second, and then:
"That's good, Daddy. Growth is good. Even when it's messy."

That's how Simone talked now.
With wisdom that snuck up on you.
With compassion that didn't coddle.

I was proud of her.
Always had been.

But I don't think I'd told her that enough.

"I'm proud of you, Simone," I said, before I could second-guess it.

She paused again. "Thank you. That means more than you probably know."

We sat in the silence for a beat.
Not uncomfortable. Just present.

Then she said, "Hey... I might be heading to Huntsville in a few weeks. If I do, I want to come by. See the space again."

"Yeah?" I said, my chest rising a little.

"Yeah. I think it's time."

"Okay," I said. "Let me know when you lock it in."

"I will. Get some sleep, Daddy."

"You too, Simone."

"Love you."

"Love you more."

The call ended, but I didn't move right away.

I sat with the weight of her voice.
The fullness of that call.
The way it didn't try to fix me—just find me.

We're on the way.
All of us.

And some days, that's enough.

Chapter 5: "Who Loves You More" — Phonte

"I tried to change my ways and pray that maybe I can save my life."

I never liked sleeping in other people's arms.

Too much room for vulnerability.
Too many angles for disappointment.

But somehow, when Alexis laid her hand across my chest that morning,
I didn't flinch.
I didn't shift.
I just breathed into it.

That was new.

She was still asleep when I woke up.
Breathing steady. Face relaxed. Her braids splayed across my pillow like sunrays.

I watched her for a while—felt a little guilty for doing so—but I couldn't help it.
She looked *whole*.
And I didn't feel like I was taking up space I hadn't earned.

I didn't want to ruin that feeling by moving too fast or talking too much.
So I laid there and tried to memorize what peace looked like.

I thought about how many years I'd spent trying to prove I was worth staying for.

Not just to women.
To myself.
To anyone who ever made me feel like love had conditions.

There was a time when I thought the work I did was how I earned my place in the world.
If I gave enough, helped enough, showed up enough—I wouldn't be left behind.

I don't know when that stopped being my religion.
Maybe around the time Darius died.
Maybe when Rhonda left.
Maybe when I ran out of excuses for why I couldn't just... be loved.

Alexis stirred beside me, opened her eyes slow, met mine with a half-smile like we'd been mid-conversation all night.

"You okay?" she asked.

"Yeah," I said out of habit. Then, more honest: "I don't know."

She didn't press.

She just let the silence hold me up.

"I ever tell you I used to make mixtapes?" I said, needing something lighter to tether me.

"Of course you did," she said, smiling. "You still have that energy."

"Nah, I mean real ones. Cassettes. Meticulously curated. Custom intros. I used to try and pack a whole conversation in a side A."

She laughed, voice still a little raspy with sleep. "What were you trying to say?"

I exhaled. Looked up at the ceiling.

Then I said it.

"That I was worth loving. Even if I didn't know how to ask for it."

She reached for my hand. Not performative. Not comforting. Just… connection.

I stared at our fingers, laced now.

It wasn't a big gesture. But it felt like a door had opened.

"There's a song I used to put on damn near every tape. Didn't matter the mood. Happy, sad, in between. I played this record a million times—"

"Just hoping they'd play it once," she said, finishing the thought.

I turned to look at her.

That moment?

That *right there?*

That's when I realized she'd been listening to me since day one.

Not just my words.
My pauses.
My silences.

"I think I'm scared of being chosen," I said, softer than I meant to.
It came out too clean, too clear.

She didn't blink.

"Then let's not call it that," she said. "Let's just… stay here. See what love feels like when you don't have to earn it."

I wanted to cry. Didn't.
But I held her hand tighter than I needed to.

Because that morning, I finally felt like I could stay.

Not because I was fixed.
Not because I'd arrived.
But because she saw all my broken edges and didn't try to sand them down.

I'd been playing the same emotional tape for years.

Trying to revise old pain with better behavior.
Trying to pray my way into being good enough.

But maybe the saving wasn't in the fixing.

Maybe it was in the **being seen**.

"I tried to change my ways and pray that maybe I can save my life."

Some mornings, it feels like I already have.

Chapter 6: "Prototype" — OutKast

"I hope that you're the one / If not, you are the prototype."

Friday night was nothing fancy.

Chinese takeout.
Couch.
Her bare feet under one of my old quilts.
And *Brown Sugar* playing in the background, mostly for the vibe.

She didn't try to talk over it. Didn't narrate or poke holes in the plot.
She just leaned into me slowly, like her body trusted mine without permission slips.

And I thought:
If forever felt like this, I'd say yes without blinking.

Here's what you need to know about Alexis:

She is **real** in a way most people forget how to be.

Not performative.
Not curated.
Just *present.*

When she laughs, it's deep—from her belly, like something was set free.
When she listens, she locks in. No scrolling. No waiting for her turn to talk.
And when she moves, she moves like she owns her space—but never makes yours feel smaller.

She's beautiful. Let me say that plain.

And not in the lazy way people throw that word around.
Alexis is the kind of beautiful that *compels you to be honest*.

Her skin is warm brown, like the inside of a pecan shell.
Her eyes carry stories—big, deliberate, softly lined with something knowing.
And her mouth? It's always doing something smart.
Smirking. Questioning. Holding back a joke she knows will land.

But none of that touches what really sets her apart.

She's beautiful because she's **anchored**.
She doesn't move just to be seen.
She *knows* who she is—and being around her makes you want to know yourself better, too.

Saturday started with music.

Not from the speakers—*from her.*
Singing under her breath in the kitchen while flipping
pancakes,
off-key and unbothered.

I stood in the doorway, arms crossed, just…
watching.
Not in awe, exactly. Just in stillness.

She had on another one of my old tees—De La Soul
this time.
Too big.
Sleeves hanging past her elbows.
Looked better on her than it ever did on me.

I didn't say anything for a while.

Didn't want to interrupt the peace she was humming
into my house.
**Our house, really—though she don't even know
it yet.**

And I loved the way she trusted me.
With her mornings.
With her softness.
With her body.

She didn't carry herself like she had to protect it from
me.

She offered closeness without calculation.
And let me move inside that trust like it was sacred
ground.

It was never just physical.
Not with her.
Not for me.

It was something quieter. Something holy.
The kind of intimacy you don't brag about.
You just hold it with both hands and thank God you
didn't fumble it.

We walked to the farmer's market after breakfast.
It wasn't planned.
She saw something online about a Black-owned
honey vendor, and ten minutes later we were outside
with hoodies on and canvas bags slung over our
shoulders.

She talked to every vendor like she knew them
already.
Asked thoughtful questions. Made eye contact.
Remembered names.

I saw myself slowing down just to keep pace with her.

Not because I couldn't keep up—
but because I didn't want to miss anything.

At one point, she handed me a mason jar full of hibiscus tea and said,
"You ever notice how nobody rushes when they're drinking out of a jar?"

I looked at her.

That's what she did to my whole damn life—
turned it into something that couldn't be rushed.

Saturday night, she danced barefoot in my living room.
Not for me.
For herself.
Headphones in, body loose, eyes closed.

I sat on the couch, watching her sway to something I couldn't hear, and I didn't need to.

Because I *saw* her.

And that was enough.

Sunday morning, we read.

No TV.
No music.
Just the rustle of pages and the occasional sound of her underlining something and saying, "Whew, read that again."

I didn't know I could fall in love with someone's
margin notes.
But here we were.

That evening, I cooked.
She sat on the counter like she always does—legs
crossed, sipping wine, giving me side commentary like
a color analyst on a quiet broadcast.

"Garlic before the greens this time?" she asked.

"I'm trying something."

"You're growing."

I smirked. "That's what you got from the garlic?"

"No," she said, smiling. "That's what I got from *you*."

After dinner, we stood at the sink, washing dishes
together.

She rinsed. I dried.

No music.
Just us.

And that's when it hit me.

Not a lightning bolt.
Not a rom-com moment.
Just a soft, certain knowing.

I looked at her—with her sleeves rolled up and her
wrists dripping with soap—and I said it in my head
first:

She's the one.

Not because she filled a void.
But because she saw every part of me that was still
healing and didn't flinch.

She challenged me without making me feel small.
She loved me without requiring me to audition for it.

"I hope that you're the one..."

I didn't just hope.

I knew.

Chapter 7: "Golden" — Jill Scott

"I'm taking my freedom, putting it in my stroll / I'll be high-steppin', y'all, letting the joy unfold..."

My phone buzzed at 6:04 a.m.

First text was from Rodney:
You still good for the meeting?

Next was from Simone:
Don't forget to hydrate. You're not 25.

Third one was from Alexis:
♫ ☻
No words. Just that. She didn't need any.

I rubbed my eyes and let out a long sigh. Today was stacked—three meetings, a tour with potential donors, Rodney's planning session, a last-minute parent sit-down, and an open mic event we forgot to post about until two days ago.

Old me would've braced for chaos.

But today?
I smiled.

Let's go.

By 7:15, I was in the building.

The Spot buzzed early on Fridays. Kids finishing up art projects. A volunteer DJ doing a sound check for the afternoon. Coffee brewing strong in the office thanks to Ms. Celeste, who didn't believe in decaf or excuses.

"Looking sharp, Patterson," she called from the hallway. "Did you iron that shirt yourself or did your lady do it?"

I chuckled, tugging at my collar. "Respectfully, I ironed it. But she picked the color."

Ms. Celeste winked. "She got good taste."

The donor tour started at 9.

Two couples, both retired educators. I walked them through the halls like I was leading them through memory—showed them where the mural lived, where the instruments were kept, where the kids wrote their verses and found their voices.

Rodney slipped into the back of the group halfway through.

Didn't say anything—just listened.

Nodded at the right moments.

Gave one of the donors a folder we didn't know we needed.

Afterward, I caught him in the stairwell.

"You really coming into your own," I said.

He shrugged. "Just following your lead."

And I didn't correct him.
But the truth?
I've been following his, too.

By lunch, I'd already forgotten I skipped breakfast.
Alexis sent another text:

**Eat. Water. Breathe.
In that order.**

I sent her back a selfie of me holding a turkey
sandwich like a trophy.
She replied with a thumbs up and a gold star.

I laughed—out loud. Right there in my office.

The planning session with Rodney and his crew ran
long, but it was electric.
Ideas flying. Music cues being debated.
A senior who'd just gotten into Spelman offered to
perform spoken word.
A freshman shyly raised her hand to volunteer to
design the flyer.

I stood by the whiteboard, letting them cook.
Letting the energy carry itself.

And I realized—
this is what legacy looks like before it gets a title.

The parent meeting that followed could've been tense—it was a disciplinary thing—but it wasn't. The mother listened, asked questions, and left the room hugging her son. I caught a glimpse of my own reflection in the glass afterward, surprised at the calm in my face.

This is what healing looks like, too.
It sneaks up on you.

The open mic was packed.
Not wall-to-wall, but enough energy to remind me why we built this place.

A ten-year-old sang Donny Hathaway.
A grandmother recited a poem she wrote for her daughter who passed.
Rodney closed the night with a piece called *"First Name Legacy."*

I damn near cried in the back row.

By the time we locked up, it was just me and the mop bucket.
One of the kids spilled punch near the rec room.

I could've left it for tomorrow.
Didn't.

Some joy you clean up for.
Some joy you preserve.

I sat on the front steps after, letting the night air hit my face.

I didn't win the lottery.
Nothing wild happened.
Nobody threw a parade.

But I felt full.

Not from food.
Not from applause.
Just from *living all the way through the day.*

I pulled out my phone and texted Alexis:
Today was golden. That's the only word for it.

Her reply came a minute later:
You're glowing. I can feel it from here.

I stayed on that step for a long while.

Letting the day settle.
Letting the joy unfold.

And for the first time in a long time, I wasn't waiting for the other shoe to drop.

I was just...

living.

Journal Entry (Later that Night)

April, late.
The Spot is finally quiet.

Today was busy, wild, packed.

But I never felt rushed.
I never felt lost.

People saw me today.
Kids, elders, Alexis, Simone.
And I didn't shrink.

This life... it's mine now.
It's not something I inherited.
It's something I've shaped.

And somehow, she keeps showing up like she was always meant to fit inside the frame.

Golden.

That's the word.

Interlude: "Something in the Way (You Make Me Feel)" — Stephanie Mills

"Something in the way you make me feel (Oh, it's something) / Feel (Yes, it's something), feel (I tell you, baby) / Something in the way you make me feel / Feel (Oh), feel (And it makes me feel real good, real good)"

The thing about Malik?

He's always thinking.

Even when he's quiet.
Even when he's laughing.
Even when he's moving through the room like it's just another day.

There's always something under the surface.
A question he hasn't asked yet.
A truth he's still working up the courage to tell.

And I don't push.

Because I don't need him to be fully healed.
I just need him to be **real**.
And he is. Without even trying.

He does this thing—
where he checks the room before he relaxes.
Not out of paranoia.
Out of habit.
Like he's making sure it's safe to exhale.

Sometimes I want to tell him:
Baby, it's safe.
You can breathe in here.
You can fall apart and I won't leave the pieces scattered.
But I don't say it yet.

I just stay.

I stay when the quiet stretches too long.
I stay when he overexplains things I already
understand.
I stay when he forgets I'm watching him become
something softer.

And when he touches me...

It's never rushed.
Never careless.
He doesn't grab—he *grounds*.

Even in the smallest moments—his hand at the small
of my back when we're walking, his palm resting
lightly on my knee when I'm mid-rant, the way he
traces my spine like he's reminding me I'm real—
there's intention in it.

Not ownership.
Presence.

A kind of "I see you, I honor you" without needing
to say a word.

There's protection in it.
Not the kind that tries to save me.
The kind that says, *You're safe here. Exactly as you are.*

He cooked for me last night.
Stood in the kitchen trying to act like it wasn't a big
deal, but I could tell he wanted it to land.

And it did.

Not because of the seasoning.
But because of the intention.

He fed me like he was trying to say something
without saying it.

There was a moment—while we were reading, Sunday
morning—
when he turned the page too fast and doubled back
like he didn't want to miss a word.

And I thought:
That's how I want to be loved.
Not perfectly.

Just attentively.
And he's doing that.

Even when he doesn't know it.

I haven't said I love him yet.

Not because I don't.
But because I want the moment to match the meaning.

And when I say it,
I want him to feel the **quiet certainty** I've been carrying for weeks.

He's not a project.
He's not a placeholder.

He's a man who's learning to let someone see him whole.

And I see him.
God, I see him.

Chapter 8: "For the Cool in You" — Babyface

"Here we go 'round, and 'round, and 'round, and back, and forth, you know / Everybody goes through it sometime, and that's just the way it flows."

It had been just under a month since that golden day. The kind of day you don't realize is a turning point until the light doesn't leave you.

Things didn't slow down. If anything, life picked up speed. The Spot was buzzing like a stereo left on low volume—constant, background life humming in every corner.

Rodney's benefit showcase was less than two weeks out. Rehearsals were happening in layered waves: music in one room, poetry being workshopped in another, the tech crew arguing (politely) over light transitions and mic feedback.

Simone confirmed she was coming to town that weekend. Alexis started showing up more regularly— not just at my place, but at The Spot too—helping kids brainstorm event names, passing out snacks, laughing with Ms. Celeste like they were cousins instead of near-strangers.

And me?

I'd started to walk like I belonged to something.

I didn't even notice it until Gerald said it during one of our calls.

"You moving different, boy. Sound lighter. Like you finally dropped the old bags and picked up something worth carrying."

He meant it as a compliment, even if it came with that Gerald-style gruffness. And he wasn't wrong.

It was a Saturday. Mid-afternoon. Warm, but not heavy. One of those days where the sun feels like it's got manners.

Alexis and I were walking through a pop-up market downtown. Local vendors, vinyl crates, small-batch lemonade and the smell of barbecue and shea butter in the same breeze.

She wore her **gold hoops,** the ones that brushed her collarbone.

The same ones she wore the first day I met her at The Spot.
The day she came in with her calm voice and big vision, asking about volunteer opportunities.
The day she surprised me just by being exactly who she was.

She had on a black tee and jeans that day. Just like now.
No frills, no presentation—just presence.

We moved through the crowd easily, not rushed. Every now and then she'd pause to flip through records or chat with someone she knew. I didn't mind. Watching her in her element was like watching a jazz solo—improvised, intentional, and way smoother than anything I could fake.

She held up a Roy Ayers vinyl at one table. "You know this one?"

I nodded. "Come on now. That's essential listening."

"Just checking. Gotta make sure you're still qualified."

I leaned in close, enough for her to feel my smirk more than hear it.

"I'm certified, Alexis. Stamped and verified. I don't need one of those corny blue checks people pay for just to feel seen."

She laughed loud enough for a few heads to turn, then tucked the record under her arm like it belonged to her already.

"Good," she said, "'cause I don't do weak credentials."

Later, we sat on a park bench near a food truck. Split a plate of fries. Her ankle rested against mine casually, like it knew something before we did.

"You ever think about legacy?" I asked, almost without thinking.

She chewed thoughtfully, then wiped her fingers. "All the time. Not in a pressure way, more in a... leave-the-door-open-behind-you kind of way."

I nodded slowly. That sounded like her. Intentional. Quietly expansive.

"You?" she asked.

"Yeah. More lately. Watching Rodney become Rodney. Seeing Simone step into herself. It's like... I want to do right by where I came from and who's coming next."

She squeezed my hand.

We sat in silence, the good kind. The kind that fills in the gaps without needing to speak.

That night, she stayed over.

We didn't do anything grand. No fancy dinner. No playlist curated for romance.

Just a shared toothbrush cup. A little back-and-forth teasing while folding laundry. Her in one of my hoodies, curled up reading while I sat at the foot of the bed finishing up notes for the benefit program.

At one point she looked up from her book and said, "You're cool, you know that?"

I looked over. "Cool how?"

She shrugged. "In the way you carry things. In how you touch. In how you let people feel safe around you without making it a thing."

I didn't say anything for a beat. Then: "You make it easier. To be like that."

She smiled, wide and soft.

And I knew. Again.

Whatever this was?

It was built for staying.

Even the cool in me had roots now.

Chapter 9: "Love Is You" — Chrisette Michele

"Love is kind when the world is cold / Love stays strong when the fight gets old / Love's a shoulder to lean on, love is you."

The day started slow.

No calendar reminders. No urgent texts from Rodney. No deadlines knocking at the door.

Just sunlight spilling across the floor and the scent of coffee drifting in from the kitchen.

I stood in that quiet for a while, barefoot, hoodie on, wondering how long it had been since I let a morning greet me instead of sprinting past it. Felt like the air had a softness to it I hadn't known in years. A warmth not just from the sun, but from being still.

Alexis was already in the kitchen, barefoot too. She moved easy, humming something soft. Not a song I recognized, but something that had her shoulders swaying. She had flour on her hands and a smudge on her cheek, like the morning had been working on her, too.

She didn't know I was watching.

And I didn't need to interrupt the peace she was creating just by being in my home.

Our home. At least that's how it felt today.

She turned slightly, caught me in the doorway, and grinned. "You always stare like that when you first wake up?"

"Only when I've got a view like this," I said.

She shook her head, but I saw the smile tuck itself deeper into her cheeks.

Later, we sat on the front steps, coffees in hand, wrapped in the kind of silence that doesn't ask to be filled.

"I ever tell you my mother used to say love shows up most when you're not trying to perform it?" I said.

Alexis looked over at me, eyes warm. "She was right."

I nodded. "You do that. Show up without trying to prove anything. It took me a while to see it for what it is."

She didn't say thank you. Just rested her head on my shoulder.

That meant more.

Because I've known loud love. Love that needed witnesses. Love that always needed proving.

But this?
This was grown. Quiet. Intentional.

That afternoon, I stopped by The Spot. Rodney was running a music sorting session, cataloging vinyl donations. A few of the teens were lounging in the corner, headphones on, debating Tribe vs. De La like it was sacred.

One of the kids handed me a record to file. *Songs in the Key of Life.*

"This the one, right?" she asked.

I nodded. "That's the blueprint."

She grinned and slid it into place.

Another kid chimed in, "You think love's like music? Like, it has eras and moods and stuff?"

I laughed. "I think real love is more like the bassline. You don't always notice it first, but everything depends on it."

They nodded like that made sense.

And something about that cracked something open in me. That I could be standing here, surrounded by kids searching for themselves in sound, in rhythm, in memory—and not feel like I had to control it. Just hold the space for it.

That felt like love, too.

Back home, Alexis had dinner almost ready.

"I didn't go overboard," she said, "just made what I had."

I looked at the table—baked salmon, greens, jasmine rice, cornbread.

"You call this casual?"

She smiled. "I cook when I'm happy."

"I could get used to that," I said.

She didn't reply. Just kissed me on the cheek and kept stirring the pot like she didn't just undo me with that one gesture.

We ate slow. We talked about everything and nothing. We cleaned up without dividing tasks. No scorekeeping. No "I did this, now you do that." Just movement in sync.

Afterward, while she changed into one of my oversized tees, I stayed in the kitchen a while longer and let the moment settle.

Then I wrote this down in my journal:

Love is not loud.
Love is not a question I keep asking in different
rooms.
Love is the answer I keep living into.
Love is the way she stands in my kitchen like it
belongs to her.
Love is the silence that doesn't demand to be
broken.

Before bed, she pulled the covers up around her
shoulders and looked at me for a long moment.

"You good?" she asked.

"Yeah," I said. "You?"

She nodded. "Yeah. This feels like something I can
believe in."

That stayed with me long after the lights were off.

That love could be something we *believe in*.

Not just fall into.
Not just survive.
But trust.

Like truth beyond fear.
Like joy inside tears.
Like her.

Love is her.
Love is you.

Chapter 10: "Euphorium (Back to the Light)" — Phonte

"Been feeling real good man, when I see myself / First time in my life feeling like I can finally be myself."

I woke up that morning with no weight on my chest.

No knot in my stomach. No old shadows tugging at the edge of my peace.

Just me.

In my bed. In my space. In my body.

And I felt good.

Not euphoric like fireworks and confetti—just clear. Grounded. Like I'd finally stepped into a version of myself that didn't apologize for existing.

I didn't even reach for my phone right away. No scrolling. No news. Just me and the light drifting in slow through the blinds.

That used to feel like a luxury. Now it felt like a right.

I showered with music on. A playlist I hadn't touched in months. Slum Village. Erykah. Then Phonte's

"Euphorium" came on, and I just stood there in the steam, letting that line wash over me:

"Been feeling real good man, when I see myself / First time in my life feeling like I can finally be myself."

I said it out loud.

Then I said it again.

And I meant it.

At The Spot, the energy matched mine.

Rodney had the stage taped off in perfect symmetry, measuring things twice like an engineer. He'd grown more focused lately—not just responsible, but invested. You could see the pride in the way he moved, the way he took care of things. The boy was starting to move like a man.

The poets were in the back room workshopping their lines. A few of the dancers were testing out floor space. Kids were drawing posters. And Ms. Celeste was already deep in logistics mode—clipboard in hand, rattling off snack needs like we were feeding an army.

It was chaos. But it was beautiful. It was **ours**.

Alexis showed up around noon, fresh off a site visit. She still had her tablet in hand and that little line between her eyebrows she got when she was in deep focus. I could tell she'd been solving something all morning.

"You eat?" she asked before she even said hello.

"No."

She handed me a sandwich and a look. "Fix that."

I smiled, bit into it. She kissed my cheek without stopping and kept walking toward the back room. That's how we were now—in rhythm. No ceremony. Just instinct.

I watched her for a second longer than I meant to.

Not because she looked good—though she always did—but because she belonged here. She folded into the community like she'd always been a part of it. She didn't have to try. She just *fit*.

Rodney caught me a little later. "You good for this weekend? You ready?"

I nodded. "Yeah. You?"

He grinned. "I been ready."

And he had. He was owning his space now. Not trying to impress. Just being who he was.

There was something special about watching him grow. It felt like watching Darius stretch his legs in another lifetime. Same confidence. Same stubborn smile. Same undercurrent of genius, still learning how to rise.

He didn't know it, but I was already proud of him. Had been.

And in a way that surprised me—I was proud of myself, too.

That night, back home, I took out my journal again.

I didn't write about fears. Or what-ifs. Or regrets.

I wrote:

Today, I was full.
Today, I didn't rehearse being okay. I just was.
Today, I showed up and stayed.
Today, I didn't feel like I had to earn my peace. I just let it in.
Today, I felt like the man I used to hope I'd become.

I paused.

And for a moment, I thought about Mama. I thought about how she'd smile seeing me still. Not chasing. Not breaking.

Just living.

Then I put the pen down and just sat there.

No need to chase light.

I was already in it.

Interlude: "Verses From Tampa"

I lit the candle on my desk like I always do when I'm about to write something that matters.

Lavender. Eucalyptus. Same playlist in the background—Hi-Tek, Blu, a little Noname, some Common for good measure. A Tribe Called Quest instrumental slid in next, and I grinned.

Daddy would like that.

The city outside was loud, even this late. Sirens echoing through humid air, someone's bassline bleeding from a car window four floors below.

But my room was still. Sacred.

I sat on the edge of my bed with the notebook in my lap.

Not my planner. Not my school journal. The *real* one. The Ms. Metaphor one. The one I don't keep on any drive. The one with the tape on the spine and the pages that smell like ink and memory.

I touched the corner of the page like it might fold into something holy.

Then I wrote:

Some folks teach you with a heavy hand,
You taught me with a heavy heart,
That beat steady like a bassline,
Even when the rhythm fell apart.

I paused, tapping the pen against my thigh. Then I flipped back a few pages and read what I'd scribbled last week:

He ain't say my name, but he raised me right,
Even in silence, Pops taught me how to fight.

That one still hits.

I closed my eyes and saw him again—not as the serious man from my childhood, but as the man I spoke to last week. Softer. Slower. Still trying, but *real*.

We don't say everything. We're both built like that.

But I know he hears me now. I feel it in the pause before he answers. The space he makes for me to step in fully.

He still doesn't know I'm Ms. Metaphor.

But he will.

I flipped to a new page and started again:

Got your patience in my pause,
Your fire in my frame,
Every metaphor I drop,
You there between the flame.

And that's the truth.

Whether he knows it or not.

Chapter 11: "Joy and Pain" — Maze feat. Frankie Beverly

"Joy and pain / Like sunshine and rain..."

Dad called before I had the chance to call him.

Which, if you know him, you know how rare that is.

"Boy, you still alive?" he asked, before I could even say hello.

"Last I checked," I said. "What's good, Dad?"

"Just making sure you didn't fall in love and forget how to use a phone."

I chuckled. "Nah, I'm here."

I was sitting on the back steps of The Spot, sun low, warmth still clinging to the air. The air smelled like early evening—barbecue somewhere in the distance, car exhaust, that fresh pine cleaner Celeste always overuses.

Dad's voice sounded brighter than usual. Not cheerful, just... unguarded.

"You got a minute?" he asked. "I was gonna play something for you."

"You? Play music over the phone?"

"Don't start with me. Just listen."

A few seconds of static. Then it came through the speaker—smooth, confident, unmistakable.

Maze. Frankie Beverly. "Joy and Pain."

I closed my eyes and let it hit.

He didn't say anything else. Just let the song play.

"That take you back?" he finally asked, a little gravel in his voice now.

"Yeah," I said. "I remember you cleaning the Monte Carlo with that on blast. Sunday mornings. White tank top. Brown liquor in a glass you called iced tea."

He laughed, deep and genuine. "That was iced tea. Mind your business."

We both sat with that laugh a little longer than necessary.

"Had that tape on repeat," he said. "Wore it out."

"You ever get tired of it?" I asked.

"Nah. Song told the truth."

We talked for a while after that. Not heavy stuff. Just music. Cars. Rodney. Alexis. He asked if I was sleeping okay. Eating enough. I asked if he was still working on that old Cutlass. He said he was thinking about selling it, but we both knew he wasn't.

There was a pause.

"You know," he said, voice lower now, "I didn't always get the balance right."

"What do you mean?"

He cleared his throat. "I did the 'supposed to' stuff. Kept the lights on. Paid what needed paying. Didn't miss work. But... I didn't always live. Not really."

I didn't say anything. Just listened.

"That song?" he said. "Joy and pain. That's how it goes. But I was scared of the joy part. Figured it wouldn't last, so I didn't trust it."

"And now?" I asked.

He exhaled. "Now I watch you. And I see you actually living. And it makes me think maybe I should've learned how."

I didn't expect that.

Not from him.

I wanted to say something, but I was too caught up in what he'd already said. So I just let the silence stretch.

He filled it anyway.

"I'm proud of you."

It hit different this time.

"Thanks, Dad."

"I mean it. You building something. And you ain't just talking about it. You doing it."

After another beat, I said, "You know, sometimes I feel like we didn't know how to be in the same room until we both got quiet enough to hear each other."

He let out a soft laugh. "That's about right."

The song was still looping behind us.

Joy and pain.
Like sunshine and rain.

"I used to think that song was about heartbreak," I said.

Dad grunted. "It is. But not the kind people think. It's about living long enough to know both things come together. You don't get one without the other. If you try to dodge pain, you dodge joy too."

"Sounds like something Mama would've said," I offered.

"Probably where I learned it. Too late, but still."

We sat with that.

Two men, not perfect. But trying.

A little more healed than yesterday.

A little more whole than we thought we were allowed to be.

We hung up a few minutes later. Nothing dramatic. Just a, "Alright then," and a click.

But I stayed on those back steps a while longer.

The sun was gone, but the warmth hadn't left.

And neither had his words.

Not perfect. Not patched.

Present.

And that's what love looks like sometimes.

Just a man trying to reach his son.

And a son finally answering.

Chapter 12: "Simply Beautiful" — Al Green

"If I gave you my love / I'd tell you what I'd do / I'd expect a whole lot of love out of you."

The call came in mid-morning.

I missed it.

I was at The Spot, helping Rodney reset folding chairs after a scheduling mess with the dance team. My phone buzzed in my pocket, but I ignored it.

Later, in a quiet moment, I saw it.

Voicemail from Dad.

He never left voicemails.

I pressed play.

"Hey. Just thinking about something, and I didn't wanna wait to say it. Been listening to records this morning. You know— old man rituals. Coffee. Dusty vinyl. Got to Al Green."

There was a pause. A little static. The sound of him shifting in his chair.

And then... he started humming.

Not clumsily. Not jokingly.

Soft. Tuned. Real.

Then, in a voice I hadn't heard in my entire life, he started to sing—quietly but steady:

"You're simply beautiful... yeah, yeah... simply beautiful..."

And he sounded good. Not like a polished singer— but like a man who used to sing when he believed he had something worth singing for.

My heart paused.

"She used to love this one," he said, voice lower now. "Played it every Saturday while she cleaned. Said it made the house smell better."

He laughed once, soft and short. A sound full of memory.

"I used to play it back for her when she'd let me. When we was good. When we wasn't sayin' all the wrong things. That song always brought her back to me—even when we were far."

Another pause. The record skipped faintly in the background.

"I figured you should know. She wasn't just your mama, you know. She was mine too. Still is, some days. That song was hers, but she let me hold it sometimes."

Click.

That was it.

But it stayed with me like a sermon.

I sat down on the edge of the stage and listened to the message again.

And again.

I'd always thought of Mama as mine. My anchor. My ache. My origin story.

But he had loved her too. Not just because he was supposed to—but in the way men do when they don't always have the words, just the records that say them better.

She was part of him.
And he still missed her.

That afternoon, Dad called back.

This time, I picked up.

"You get my message?"

"I did," I said, voice thick.

There was silence for a second.

"She would've liked Alexis."

That caught me off guard. "What?"

"I mean it. She had that way of sensing people. Would've known right away. And I'm not her, but I see it too. You different now. You softer around her. Still you—but... more."

I let that settle.

"Dad," I said, "you sure about all this?"

He laughed. "Boy, I'm seventy-three. You think I got time to *not* be sure?"

I exhaled into a smile. "Fair."

"I wanna meet her."

"You do?"

"Yeah. Not tomorrow. Not next week. But yeah—I do. And tell Simone too. That song—Al Green— that's part of her, too. Pass it down. Let her know where the sweetness came from."

After we hung up, I moved quiet through the rest of my day.

Not sad. Not shaken.

Softened.
Grounded.
Full.

That night, I sent Simone a text.

This was your grandmother's favorite song. I just found out today.
Listen when you're still. It carries something.

Attached was the link to *"Simply Beautiful."*

Then I called Alexis.

She answered on the second ring. "Hey."

I didn't say a word.

I just played the song.

Held the phone close to the speaker. Let Al Green do what Al Green does.

She didn't interrupt. She knew exactly what it meant.

When the song ended, I still didn't speak for a moment.

Then:
"I miss you."

Not needy. Not dramatic.

Just **true**.

She exhaled into the phone. "I know."

I smiled.

"Goodnight, babe."

"Goodnight."

Interlude: "Spaces Between"

Alexis.
The hotel room was quiet.
Too quiet.
Not the kind of quiet she got when Malik was lost in his thoughts, or writing something in that small black journal he never let her peek into.
This quiet was hollow.

She reached for her charger and caught herself reaching for his hand instead.
She laughed.
Turned the lamp off.
Whispered goodnight to nobody.
Fell asleep with his song still looping in her chest.

Malik.
There was a little pause in the way the house sounded when she wasn't in it.
A mug left in the exact spot she always put it.
Her scarf still hanging on the back of the chair.
He could still smell her conditioner in the bathroom.

He didn't call her.
Didn't text right away.
Just let the day pass and caught himself talking to her in his head twice before noon.

He smiled to himself.
He missed her in that grown-up way—where absence wasn't pain, just an echo of presence.

Simone.
She played Jill Scott's *"Whenever You're Around"* for the third time in a row.
Let it play through the Bluetooth speaker in her bedroom, the volume just loud enough to fill the corners.

"'Cause I'm lonely whenever you're around…"

That line took her straight back.

Back to age twelve.
Sitting at the kitchen table doing homework. Malik at the other end—home, but not really there. Quiet. Distant.
Answering questions with half-smiles and nods.
She remembered wishing he would just *see her*. Ask her something that mattered. Let her in.

That ache was real.

And even though their relationship had grown since then… sometimes it still lingered.

She paused the song, picked up a pen.

In the notebook marked **PRIVATE**, she started a new page.

"Dear Dad,
There are things I want to say.
About who I am.
About what I've built.
And who I love..."

She stopped writing.

Looked over at the framed photo of her and Maya from that weekend in Asheville—wind in their faces, heads leaning into each other like they were holding up the same piece of sky.

"She's part of the story, too," she whispered.

Rodney.
He hung back after rehearsal and picked up chairs nobody told him to fold.

He saw one of the younger kids struggling with a verse and offered to help.

Didn't raise his voice.

Didn't ask for attention.

Just moved like somebody who'd been taught to show up.

Chapter 13: "Whenever You're Around" — Jill Scott

"Cause I'm lonely whenever you're around."

The morning came quiet.

I made my coffee slow. Let the water boil instead of rushing the process. Watched it swirl in the pot like time was mine to keep.

The kitchen was still. No humming from the other room. No sound of her bare feet brushing against the tile. No playful shade thrown over her shoulder while she dug for the right mug.

Just silence.

I missed her.

Not in a way that made me anxious or uncertain.

In a way that settled behind my ribs and stayed there.

She was in Atlanta—urban planning conference, networking, site visits. The kind of thing she was built for. Vision, design, community. She moved with purpose.

And I was proud of her.

But I missed her.

I poured my coffee into the mug she always reached for—the tall navy one with the chip near the handle.

She'd call it *"seasoned."* Said the best mugs had a little story in them.

I sat at the table and scrolled through emails I didn't really want to read. Answered a couple of texts. Left a few unanswered just because.

The house felt like it was holding its breath.

And so was I.

I walked through the house with my coffee, not even trying to fill the space she usually held. Her presence had a weight that was more spirit than sound. When she was gone, it echoed.

The plants looked like they missed her, too.

Her throw blanket, her scarf on the chair, her open book on the edge of the couch.

It felt like the space still remembered her shape.

I stood in the doorway to the bedroom for a beat longer than I should have.

The covers still carried her imprint.

And for a second, I saw her there—head wrapped, face softened by sleep, lips curved just enough to remind me that peace had a body.

I stepped outside, leaned against the porch rail, and let the morning roll by slow.

In my head, I heard her laugh.

In my chest, I felt the silence she'd left.

Funny thing is, I used to crave quiet. Now I know the difference between silence that heals and silence that hollows.

I opened a note on my phone. Thought about sending her something. Thought about saying what I was thinking out loud.

But it didn't feel like a text moment.

This wasn't emojis and clever lines.

This was... *her.*

And the ache of her not being here.

I typed something. Deleted it. Then just closed the screen.

Later that afternoon, I drove over to The Spot. Just to be around rhythm. Movement. Sound. Something that breathed on its own.

Rodney was in the back with a few of the teens, workshopping flow and delivery.

He nodded at me but didn't call me over. He was in his element.

Celeste waved, muttered something about needing to reorder snacks.

The Spot was living. And that grounded me.

I sat in the main room, alone, speakers off. The space held me like it knew something was missing, too.

I scrolled through playlists, not really looking for anything, until I saw it.

Jill Scott — "Whenever You're Around."

I hit play.

The beat wrapped around me soft and deliberate.

Her voice floated in.

And that line:

"'Cause I'm lonely whenever you're around."

It hit different.

Not because Alexis made me feel that way. Not anymore.

But because I knew that feeling.

I knew what it was like to want someone so present you could feel their absence before they even left the room.

And I wondered if that was how Simone once felt about me.

I thought about all the ways I used to dodge presence.

How I kept people close but not in.

How I stood in doorways but never stepped through.

How I let rooms go cold and called it survival.

I let the song play through.

Then I played it again.

Just to sit with the silence it left behind.

And to remind myself: the next time she was near me, I would hold her longer.

Not tighter. Just longer.

Because some people leave a light behind when they walk away.

And I wanted to be the man who didn't take that light for granted.

Simone

She replayed her dad's voicemail from the day before—not because he'd said anything monumental, but because of what he hadn't.

There was warmth in his voice. Like he'd started to understand how to speak *to her*, not just *at her*.

She sat cross-legged on the floor, Maya behind her, twisting the ends of her curls with the kind of intimacy that softened the air.

"You thinking about telling him soon?" Maya asked.

Simone nodded. "Yeah. I think he's ready to see me. All of me."

Maya smiled, but her hands slowed just a little.

"I haven't told my folks," she said. "Not yet."

That small silence after—Simone knew that sound. A door easing shut.

Maya kissed her shoulder. "It's not about hiding you. It's about not wanting to fight with them."

Simone didn't push.

She just picked up her notebook and flipped to a blank page.

Something in her was starting to stir.

Ms. Metaphor.

Not as performance.

As clarity.

As truth in motion.

The pen tapped once against the paper, then started to move.

"What if I wrote the mirror / Spoke the flame / Rhymed the name / Not the mask?"

A new piece was being born.

Not a verse to hide in.

A verse to *arrive* in.

Alexis

She woke to sunlight in slivers and her phone buzzing once.

A message.

From him.

Malik never sent selfies. Not even once.

But here it was.

His face, just slightly tilted. No smile. Just eyes that looked like *home.*

The caption read:

If I can't be there, this is the next best thing. Just so you know—I'm still right here.

She didn't respond right away.

She just stared at it.

And said out loud to no one, "You've been here the whole time."

Alexis leaned back into the pillow, pressed the phone to her chest, and let her breath catch.

She missed her man.

Not with desperation.

But with depth.

She missed him the way roots miss water. The way a good song misses a skipped verse.

And he had sent himself, the only way he knew how.

A picture.
A presence.
A promise.

Chapter 14: "Love Me Still" — Chaka Khan

"I've wandered far, I've had my fill / I need you now, do you love me still?"

There's a kind of peace that don't come easy.

You have to fight for it, then let it find you anyway.

That's where I was.

Not perfect. Not fixed. But present. More than I'd ever been.

I was walking through my neighborhood after dinner, hands in my pockets, letting the breeze cool whatever heat the day left behind. No destination. Just movement. Just breath.

The quiet gave me space to listen to the voices I usually turned down.

Old ones. Regret. Doubt. Even shame.

And I let them talk.

But I didn't let them *drive*.

I used to be scared that if people saw all of me—the indecision, the mess, the mistakes—they'd leave.

That kind of fear runs deep. Especially when you've lost love before.

I thought about Rhonda. How we drifted. How I wasn't ready. How I thought showing my cracks meant breaking everything.

I thought about Simone. How she used to look at me like I was ten feet tall—and how I let the distance between us grow until she started filling it with poems instead of questions.

And then I thought about Alexis.

Alexis didn't try to fix me.

She didn't beg for explanations.

She let me unfold.

Layer by layer. Scar by scar.

And even in the days when I didn't have words for what I was feeling, she never walked away from the silence.

She stayed.

And in that staying, she taught me how to show up—
not just for her, but for myself.

Earlier that day, I'd come across an old record while
organizing crates for the benefit night.

Chaka Khan.

I dropped the needle just to see if it still played clean.

And when that voice came through?

*"I've wandered far, I've had my fill / I need you now, do you
love me still?"*

I had to sit down.

Because that was it.

That was the truth I'd been circling for years.

The people who still love you after they know you?

That's rare.

Simone still called me *Dad*, even when I hadn't always
been one.

Rodney looked at me like I was someone worth
modeling, even on days I doubted myself.

My father told me he was proud.

Alexis looked at me like I was hers.

Not in possession.

In faith.

In joy.

In truth.

I walked until the sky turned that soft blue that only exists between sunset and streetlights.

The kind of sky Mama used to call "a sky that knows secrets."

I didn't listen to music. Didn't text anyone. Just let the breeze carry the sound of my own footsteps.

And for the first time in a long time, I didn't need forgiveness to feel whole.

I just needed to believe I was loved.

Still.

I didn't hear her come in at first.

Just the sound of keys, and the low squeak of the front door as it shut behind her.

Then the softest voice from down the hall.

"Hey, baby."

I turned from the kitchen sink, hands still wet from rinsing a plate I didn't really need to clean.

She walked in, travel-worn and still beautiful in the way only she could be—hair up, hoops still on, hoodie slightly oversized. My hoodie.

We didn't rush.

She didn't drop her bag right away.

We just looked at each other for a few seconds longer than usual.

Then I stepped across the floor and pulled her into me.

No need to talk.

She leaned her head against my chest and let her hands settle at the small of my back.

"You good?" I whispered.

She nodded.

"You?"

"I am now."

She stayed wrapped in my arms for a while.

Long enough for her scent to fill the space again.

Long enough for me to remember that sometimes the most radical thing a man can do is *stay open*.

Chapter 15: "Get It Together" — Beastie Boys ft. Q-Tip

"Got to get it together and see what's happening."

The Spot was humming before I even opened the front door.

You could feel it in the sidewalk. In the bass leaking out of the building. In the energy of kids coming and going, swapping inside jokes and passing around flyers like currency.

Something was happening.

And it wasn't chaos—it was *orchestration.*

The place had a rhythm now. A heartbeat.

And I wasn't the only one keeping it steady.

Rodney was already inside, moving fast, clipboard in one hand, earbuds in. He didn't see me walk in. He was too busy pointing out stage dimensions with one of the lighting techs who looked way too serious for a community benefit.

I didn't interrupt. I just stood in the entrance for a minute, soaking it in.

The banners were hung. Folding chairs lined up like they had something to say. Celeste was directing volunteers like she was running a live broadcast. Tables were labeled. Vendors were setting up early. The DJ had his crates lined and color-coded.

This wasn't just a center anymore.

This was a production.

A movement.

Celeste caught my eye from across the room and gave me a nod.

"I told you he was built for this," she said, handing me a box of programs fresh from the printer. "Don't act surprised."

"I'm not surprised," I said. "Just… watching."

"Good. Then move that box. Watching ain't work."

Rodney finally spotted me, pulled out one earbud, and made his way over.

"You see the schedule?" he asked, handing me a folded paper with too many moving parts and barely any white space.

I scanned it. Music. Dance. Spoken word. A community panel. Local artists. Food trucks. A short film screening. Even a table for voter registration.

He wasn't just putting on a show. He was building **culture**.

"This is solid," I said, and meant it.

He looked down and half-shrugged. "Just wanted it to mean something."

"It does," I said. "You did that."

Right then, one of the interns hit play on a playlist to test the sound system.

A voice spilled out of the speakers.

Not loud, not flashy. But clean. Confident. Controlled.

Ms. Metaphor.

Rodney tilted his head toward the speaker and grinned.

"She's ill, right?"

I nodded slowly.

There was a line—quick, but razor sharp—that caught me off guard:

"Don't wait for the world to clap / Build the stage, then take it back."

It echoed in my chest.

Something about her cadence. Her tone. Her intentionality.

I'd heard her name before, a few times. Seen her popping up in underground lists, passed around by the teens and a few of the younger volunteers.

But now?

Now I was *listening*.

"You nervous?" I asked Rodney.

He shook his head. "Nah. Just focused."

I nodded. "Feels like we're turning a corner."

He smiled. "Feels like we're turning the whole block."

Just as I was about to step outside to give the team room to work, I heard her voice behind me.

"Tell him the sign doesn't need to be perfect—it just needs to be straight."

Constance.

Standing by the main door with a paintbrush in one hand and a bundle of flyers in the other, laughing with one of the younger volunteers who clearly didn't know who he was getting light-heartedly checked by.

Rodney turned around and grinned. "Ma…"

"I'm just sayin'," she said, walking up beside him and handing off the flyers. "Straighten it out and keep it moving. We got people to impress."

She turned to me and smiled. "Hey, Malik."

"Hey," I said, smiling back. "You back here giving out orders?"

"Only the ones worth listening to."

Rodney shook his head but he was smiling.

There was love in it—*all of it.*

And not just mother-son love.

It was the kind of love that still held room for Darius.

Still honored him.

Still spoke his name in every act of care.

She pulled Rodney close and brushed his shoulder off like there was dust he couldn't see.

"You good?" she asked him.

"Yeah, Ma. We're locked in."

She looked over at me again. "He's been running point on this whole thing. Living and breathing it. You'd be proud."

I nodded. "I am."

She held my gaze for a second longer. Then she said, real quiet, "His daddy would be too."

That landed.

Soft. But heavy.

And true.

A vendor came over to ask about table placement. Rodney handled it like a pro, folding the schedule back into his hoodie pocket before diving into logistics like it was second nature.

I stepped aside, gave him space.

This wasn't a test anymore.

He wasn't just stepping into Darius's shadow.

He was stepping into his own light.

I looked around the room once more.

This thing—this space I once thought I had to hold up on my own—was *alive*.

Living. Moving. Multiplying.

And all I had to do was get out the way and help it breathe.

"Got to get it together and see what's happening," I murmured, more to myself than anyone.

We were doing it.

Piece by piece. Person by person.

And we weren't just putting on a benefit.

We were building legacy.

Chapter 16: "Ms. Metaphor"

"Don't wait for the world to clap / Build the stage, then take it back."

I didn't go looking for her.

Not exactly.

I was just trying to get the lighting system sorted for the stage. One of the track lights kept flickering, and the tech guy was late. I went to the back to double check the fuses and heard Rodney in one of the practice rooms, reviewing tracks.

Not playing them.

Reviewing them. Pausing, scribbling notes. Rewinding lines. Talking back to the music like it was in conversation with him.

And the voice playing through the speaker?

That was her.

Ms. Metaphor.

I'd been hearing her name for weeks.

Passed around in conversations between the teens. On playlists during programming nights. Celeste had even mentioned her once or twice, saying one of the girls at The Spot used to quote her like scripture.

I always nodded like I was in the know.

Truth was, I hadn't sat still long enough to *really listen*.

Until now.

"They taught me silence was survival / so I rhymed to stay alive—
Now I write like breathin's my revival / every word a sign I thrive."

I froze in the doorway.

Not because the bars were clever—though they were.

Not because her flow was clean—though it was.

But because there was **something else** in it.

Something buried in her cadence. Something in the way she curved the last syllable, like the words had a second meaning only she understood.

It felt like recognition.

Rodney didn't notice me yet. He was nodding, mouthing the words. Deep into it.

And I just... watched.

Listened.

Felt something stir that I hadn't expected.

Another verse hit.

Different beat. Slower. No drums, just keys and breath.

"Tried to rhyme my way to father's eyes /
Built metaphors where memories should rise."

That one hit me in the chest like a stone.

And for a second—just a second—I was back in D.C., a summer visit years ago. Simone maybe seven, sitting cross-legged on the floor of Rhonda's living room, wearing a t-shirt too big and socks that kept slipping off her feet.

She had written a "rap."

Four lines. No real rhythm. Just words.

But the look in her eyes when she read it—serious, hopeful—like she was offering me a piece of her she wasn't sure I'd know what to do with.

I remember clapping. Saying something like, *"That's tight, baby girl."*

But I don't remember asking her what it meant.

I don't remember *listening.*

Rodney finally noticed me.

"You feelin' this one?" he asked.

"Yeah," I said. Too quick. Voice too thick.

He grinned. "She's underground, but she's startin' to get buzz. All word-of-mouth. No face out there, just the voice."

I nodded slowly, eyes on the speaker.

"Ms. Metaphor," I repeated.

He kept talking. Said he'd reached out to her team. No response yet, but he was hoping she'd pull up at the benefit. Said having her would legitimize everything.

I barely heard him.

I was staring at the floor now, not seeing it.

I was back in all the silences between phone calls. Back in all the moments when I tried to be a father but didn't always know how.

Back in that moment where I wondered:

Could it be her?

The track faded out.

Rodney looked down at his notes and I slipped out before he could ask anything else.

Walked through the hallway slow.

Let the next track start and stop in the background like it was chasing me.

Ms. Metaphor.

That voice. That weight. That *intent.*

It felt like something I should've known from the start.

And that scared me a little.

Not because it might be true.

But because... what if it was?

What if my daughter had been rhyming the truth to the world—and I was the last one to catch the beat?

Chapter 17: "The Meaning of the Name" — Gang Starr

"And all the soft silly suckers I'ma wet them /
In other words destroy, boy, and then claim my fame...
This is the meaning of the name."

I sat in my car outside The Spot, engine off, windows cracked, heat curling at the edges of the glass. Late afternoon, soft light. One of those days where the air felt too full to breathe all the way in.

I wasn't ready to walk inside.

Wasn't ready to speak.

Wasn't even ready to listen to music.

And yet...

Her voice was still in my head.

Not Simone's speaking voice—the one that called to say she was doing fine, or that she couldn't talk long.

But the *other* one.

Ms. Metaphor.

I pulled out my phone and searched for the name again.

The clips came up the way they always do when someone's on the verge of something: halfway lit, blurry, real.

No glitz. No promo tour.

Just heart in waveform.

I hit play on the first one and leaned back.

"They say daughters look like their mothers /
But I write like the fathers I rarely knew."

I closed my eyes.

That wasn't just a line.

That was a key.

To a door I didn't know I had closed.

I thought about the name Rhonda gave her. **Simone Alyse.**

It was the kind of name you hum before you say out loud.

She told me once she chose it because it sounded like strength and softness could live in the same mouth.

I hadn't thought about that in years.

I'd thought I'd given her what I could—visits, support, tuition help, a shoulder if she ever needed it. But hearing this... this *voice*... I realized I'd missed something deeper.

Not just her growth.

Her *becoming*.

Another track played.

I didn't hit pause.

Didn't fast forward.

I just let it ride.

*"Name ain't fame, it's fight—it's breath /
Legacy don't need a label, it just needs depth."*

That's when it really hit.

She wasn't just rhyming for the world.

She was rhyming **through** me.

She was building metaphors around every moment I'd ever missed. Every call I'd wrapped up too quickly. Every "That's nice" I'd offered instead of leaning in.

She was telling me the truth… in public.

While I'd been trying to earn back her trust in private.

I thought about my own name.

Malik. King.

Andre. A name passed down without ceremony, just rhythm.

Patterson.

Three words.

And the initials had become my whole journey.

MAP.

I built this whole life around the idea of guidance, direction, making sense of the path behind me.

But Simone?

She'd built a compass of her own.

And called it **Ms. Metaphor.**

One last clip. A live poem. Baltimore open mic.

No video. Just audio and crowd noise.

*"Don't ask me to be quiet if you never came close to listening /
My name is metaphor—not mistake, not missing."*

That line split me in two.

Not because it was angry.

But because it was true.

She didn't say *father.*
Didn't say *Dad.*
Didn't have to.

She'd been *saying* it this whole time.

And I'd finally learned how to hear it.

I leaned back in the seat and let the silence settle.

Didn't cry.

But I felt everything.

Like breath too big to fit in one chest.

Like awe.
Like grief.
Like pride.

All braided up into something I didn't have a name for.

My daughter had taken the thing I gave her—my distance, my imperfection, my presence too little too late—and turned it into art.

And that art had made its way back to me.

Like echo.

Like prayer.

Like *proof.*

Chapter 18: "Family Business" — Kanye West

"This is family business / And this is for the family that can't be with us."

—

The kitchen was clean. Leftovers cooling. Dishes stacked. Jazz low in the background—Robert Glasper letting the keys drift like night wind.

Alexis sat on the couch in my hoodie, legs tucked under her, thumbing through a book she wasn't really reading.

I stood across from her, phone in hand, volume low.

"Got a second?" I asked.

She looked up immediately. "Of course."

I walked over, sat beside her, pulled up the clip.

Didn't say anything. Just pressed play.

"Don't ask me to be quiet if you never came close to listening / My name is metaphor—not mistake, not missing."

Alexis didn't flinch.

Didn't tilt her head or ask *who*.

She just listened. Eyes on me the whole time.

I let it play out.

When it ended, I stared at the phone a second longer than necessary. Then I set it on the coffee table like it was something sacred.

"It's Simone," I said.

The words didn't crack.

But my voice bent around them like they mattered.

Alexis didn't rush in. Didn't fill the space with a speech or a lesson.

She just reached for my hand and held it in both of hers.

"I figured," she said softly. "From the way you've been listening lately."

I exhaled. Let my body settle.

"I don't know what to say to her."

"You already did," she said. "Just not with words yet."

I looked down, then back at her.

"She's brilliant," I said.

"She always has been," Alexis replied. "And now you know how to see it."

That was the moment.

Not because she told me what to do—but because she helped me see that the silence I'd been sitting in was *mine to fill.*

The next afternoon, I sat in my car with the engine off and the phone in my hand.

Opened my contacts.
Scrolled to Simone.
Hovered.
Closed it.
Opened it again.

Finally, I just exhaled, pressed the button, and let it ring.

"Hey, Dad."

Her voice was calm. Guarded, maybe. But not cold.

I closed my eyes at the sound of it.

"Hey, baby. You got a second?"

"Yeah. What's up?"

I didn't jump in.

Didn't drop her stage name or blurt anything out.

Just eased my way into it.

"I've been listening to a lot more music lately," I said.

"Okay," she said slowly. "You? Listening to *new* music?"

"Yeah. Rodney's been slipping me some names. One stood out."

"Who?"

I paused.

"Ms. Metaphor."

She didn't say anything right away.

Just air on the line.

"I've been playing those tracks," I said. "Heavy rotation. There's something in it. Something that sounds like…"

I let the sentence hang. I couldn't finish it without my throat closing up.

"...like something you know?" she offered.

"Yeah."

A silence settled between us. Not awkward. Not angry.

Sacred.

Like we were walking across a bridge we both built, separately.

"I'm proud of her," I said. "I don't even know her. But I'm proud."

"Yeah?" she asked, soft.

"Yeah. She's saying something. To people. About people. About... family."

Another pause.

Then her voice came through. Lower. Clearer.

"Did you figure it out?"

"I think I did."

"Okay."

"I'm not asking you to confirm it. I just want you to know... if it *is* you—I hear you now."

That's when her breath caught.

Not crying.
Not gasping.

Just that little shift—the kind you hear when
someone's holding something too long and finally lets
it go.

"I didn't hide," she said quietly.

"I know."

"I just didn't think you were ready to hear me."

"I wasn't."

Another pause.

"I am now."

And there it was.

No dramatic music.
No scripted apology.
Just clarity.

We didn't need to solve everything right there.

But we'd named it.

We'd made space for something to *start*.

—

"You working on anything new?" I asked, just to ease the tension.

She chuckled. "Always."

"Let me hear it when you're ready."

"I will," she said. "Soon."

—

We said our goodbyes like it was a regular Tuesday.

But when I hung up, I felt like I'd just been handed my *real* name again.

Like a man who'd finally earned the right to be called **Dad**.

—

Later that night, Simone sat on her small patio in Tampa, legs curled up under her, phone pressed to her cheek. The stars were hiding behind clouds, but the air was soft.

Maya's voice came through the line, warm and close, like it always did.

"He figured it out?" Maya asked.

Simone nodded, even though Maya couldn't see her. "Yeah. I didn't say it outright. But he knows. Really *knows*."

Maya was quiet a moment.

"How did it feel?"

"Like I exhaled for the first time in years," Simone said.

Another pause. Then, "I'm glad."

Simone hesitated, then said, "I want to tell him about us. And Mom too. But only if you're okay with that."

Maya didn't answer right away.

Simone gave her space.

When Maya finally spoke, her voice was steady, but soft. "I'm not there yet. Not with my family. But you... you've always been bolder than me."

"I'm only bold when I feel safe," Simone said. "And you make me feel that way."

"I love you, you know that?" Maya said, low and certain.

"I do," Simone said, smiling now. "And I love you back."

"If you're ready to tell them," Maya added, "then I want you to. Don't wait on me."

"You're not holding me back," Simone said gently. "You're helping me walk forward."

They sat in silence for a while after that. The kind of quiet that feels earned.

And in Simone's chest, something settled.

Not just the truth.

But the readiness.

Chapter 19: "Good Morning Sunshine" — Little Brother

"Imagination's not the same as truth / Be careful what your mind could lead into /
People everywhere still so few / Good morning sunshine, here's a song for you."

—

The sun was already up by the time I opened my eyes.

Soft light through the blinds. Quiet in the house. Just the hum of the fridge, the occasional creak from the cooling air vents, and Alexis breathing slow beside me.

I didn't move at first.

Didn't want to.

I just lay there, staring at the ceiling, feeling the morning stretch across my chest like a warm hand.

This was peace.

Not the loud kind. Not the kind that came from fixing everything.

Just the kind that comes from *not running.*

—

Alexis stirred, turned over slowly, and smiled without opening her eyes.

"Good morning," she whispered.

I kissed her shoulder, then her temple. "Good morning, sunshine."

She chuckled. "You corny before coffee?"

"I'm corny by design," I said. "It's part of the package."

She opened one eye, peeked at me, and stretched with a soft yawn. My hoodie—hers now, let's be real—slid down one shoulder like it knew the move by heart.

And I just… watched her.

That, right there? That did something to me.

"I ever tell you what it does to me? Seeing you in my clothes?" I said, voice low.

She turned her head and looked at me, eyes half-lidded but sharp. "You about to get inappropriate before eggs?"

"Not inappropriate. Just honest."

She raised a brow, waiting.

"There's something about it," I said. "You in my hoodie, my t-shirt… it's not just sexy. It's territorial.

Like your skin and my fabric had a conversation while we were sleeping."

She laughed, one of those low, knowing ones. "You better stop talkin' like that unless you're trying to end up late to your own day."

"Late? I'll cancel the whole day," I said. "Don't tempt me."

"Tempting you is easy," she said, shifting her leg against mine. "Keeping you upright's the hard part."

"Don't threaten me with a good time," I said, grinning now.

She rolled her eyes, pulling the covers up with dramatic flair. "You're lucky I like you."

"I'm lucky you love me," I said.

She paused, softened.

"You really are," she whispered.

And that's how the day started. Not with fireworks, not with breakthroughs.

Just love in a hoodie. And a heat you don't need to chase.

She sat up and stretched again. My hoodie slid a little more, settling soft against her skin.

"You sleep okay?" she asked.

"Better than I have in a while."

She nodded. "That's 'cause you're lighter now. You laid some stuff down."

"Feels like it."

Alexis stood, walked toward the kitchen, then looked back.

"Make some eggs while you're up, Certified Corny?"

"I'll consider it if you stop acting like this isn't our house."

She grinned over her shoulder. "You just figured that out?"

—

I made breakfast.

Simple stuff.

Scrambled eggs, toast, fruit I didn't cut fancy.

And while I was cracking eggs, my phone lit up with a text from Simone.

Simone: Morning, Dad. Just wanted to say thanks again. You good?

I stared at the screen for a second.

Then typed:

Me: Better than good. I'm proud of you. Always was. Now I *know* how to say it.

A few seconds later:

Simone: That means more than I can explain. PS — You'll get another track soon. Just for you.

I smiled. Put the phone down. Stood there barefoot on the tile floor, eggs in a pan, sunlight sliding across the counter, and thought:

This is it.

Not arrival. Not ending.

But alignment.

—

Rodney texted too, just a few minutes later.

Rodney: Yo. Confirmed two poets. Vendor count is 🔥. Got a DJ lined up with live MPC set. I'm sending you clips.

I responded with a thumbs-up and a note:

Me: Proud of you, young man. The Spot is becoming something else. You're doing it.

He replied:

Rodney: It's *ours* now.

That hit me.

Not like a speech.
Like a stamp.

A shared one.

—

Back in the kitchen, I was plating eggs when I felt her behind me—bare feet, soft breath at my shoulder, the scent of her skin waking me up all over again.

Without a word, Alexis slid her arms around my waist from behind, pulled me back just enough, and kissed the side of my neck.

Then my jaw.

Then my mouth.

It wasn't rushed. Wasn't coy.

It was *intentional.*

When she pulled back, her eyes locked with mine, playful but steady.

"That's just a preview," she said, voice low, lips brushing my cheek. "If you act right today."

I blinked, breath caught.

She patted my chest once and stepped back, grabbing her coffee like she hadn't just rewired my morning.

"Go be the Malik I know you can be," she said over her shoulder.

I watched her walk out of the room like the woman who already knew the answer.

—

A few minutes later, she returned with coffee in hand and leaned against the counter, watching me.

"You smiling at eggs now?"

"Nah," I said. "Just everything."

She looked at me, tilted her head slightly.

"What?"

"Nothing," I said, walking over to her, sliding my arm around her waist. "Just thinking I've never started a day like this before."

She raised an eyebrow. "Like what?"

"Light."

She leaned in. Let her forehead rest against mine.

"Good morning, sunshine," she said again. "Now let's keep it that way."

And we did.

Chapter 20: "I Couldn't Love You More" — Sade

"I couldn't love you more if I tried."

—

The house was quiet.

Not the kind of quiet that presses on you—but the kind that **holds** you.

Alexis had stepped out early to meet with a city official about zoning updates near The Spot. I offered to come. She waved me off. *"Let me do this. You got a full heart to stretch out this morning."*

She was right.

I sat on the edge of the bed for a long time. Just... sitting.

Didn't check my phone.
Didn't reach for music.
Didn't try to turn the silence into something else.

I just existed in it.

—

She'd left a note on the mirror in dry-erase marker, just like she always did when she left before me.

Don't burn the toast. Be the man you've already become. — A.

I stared at that sentence like it had a pulse.

It read like poetry.

Like love that didn't need a reason anymore.

—

I got dressed slowly. Made coffee. Took it out back.

The morning light was slanted just right, soft through the trees. I pulled out my journal and opened it to a blank page.

For once, the words didn't feel stuck.

I didn't need to make sense of everything.

I just needed to say it plain:

This woman loves me in a way I've never let myself be loved.
And I love her back with everything that survived the man I used to be.
I couldn't love her more if I tried.

—

I thought about how she looked last night. Not in the red dress or the heels—though Lord knows she wore both like armor and art.

I thought about how she looked when she was rinsing rice at the sink, singing under her breath, off-key and happy.

I thought about her laugh when I misquoted a lyric and she corrected me without blinking.

I thought about the way she leaned into me when the world got too loud.

And the way I leaned back, without fear of falling.

—

Later that day, she came back through the door with sunlight on her shoulders and that smile that always broke my focus.

She dropped her bag, kicked off her shoes, and walked right over to me where I was standing in the kitchen.

"You eat anything?" she asked.

"Not yet."

She nodded, pulled something from the fridge, and stood beside me.

No fanfare.
No rush.

Just a woman who loved me enough to be present and a man who finally saw that as **everything.**

"I missed you," I said.

She looked at me sideways. "You saw me four hours ago."

"I missed you anyway."

She smiled without looking up. "I love when you talk sweet. You're getting good at it."

"I've been practicing," I said.

She laughed. "No, you've been listening. That's the difference."

—

We ate in silence. The kind that speaks.

And when we finished, I reached across the table and held her hand.

No announcement. No grand gesture.

Just one truth rising to the top of everything else:

I couldn't love her more if I tried.

And I wouldn't stop trying.

Chapter 21: "For the Love of You" — The Isley Brothers

"Drifting on a memory / Ain't no place I'd rather be / Than with you."

—

Gerald didn't announce himself.

He never did.

He just texted, *"At the terminal."*

That was his version of "I'm proud of you." I got in the car.

—

He hadn't been to Huntsville in years. Not since I first came back to teach at A&M. Back then, he didn't ask many questions about why I left D.C. Or why I never returned.

Now he stepped off the shuttle with a small overnight bag and his hat tilted just right. He wore his dark brown leather jacket, the one he only pulled out when the visit *meant something.*

"Flight good?" I asked.

"They still put too many people in one tube. But yeah."

That was his version of "I'm fine."

We rode in silence for a little while. I let one of his old playlists ride—classic Isley Brothers, S.O.S. Band, Bobby Womack. Familiar ground.

Gerald tapped the dash when *"For the Love of You"* came on.

"Now this right here," he said, "this'll outlast all that trap y'all pretend to like."

I smiled.

Didn't argue.

Didn't need to.

—

When we pulled up to The Spot, he looked out the window, lips pressed, eyes scanning like he was about to appraise it—but not with numbers. With memory.

"You built this?"

"Me and the community. But yeah. It's mine."

He nodded slowly.

"You got parking."

I laughed. "High praise."

Inside, The Spot was alive. Not loud. Just humming.

Rodney was over by the main display area, helping a couple teens stack extra chairs for the upcoming open mic series. Someone was painting in the studio. A young girl walked by with a box of donated books.

Gerald looked around with a long, slow breath. He nodded—but this time it was deeper. Like he was letting something go.

Then his eyes landed on Rodney.

"Who's that?" he asked.

I smiled. "That's Rodney. Darius's son."

Gerald turned toward me a little, his eyebrows raised.

"You ain't say the boy looked just like him."

"I figured you'd see it for yourself."

Rodney noticed us and walked over.

"Pops," he said to me, dapping me up. Then he looked at Gerald. "You must be Mr. Patterson."

"Gerald," he corrected, shaking Rodney's hand. "You Darius's boy?"

"Yes sir."

Gerald held on to the handshake a second longer than expected.

Then he said, real quiet, "I see your daddy in you. In your shoulders. In your eyes."

Rodney smiled, almost bashful.

Gerald turned to me, voice softer than I expected.

"He's proud of you, Malik."

I nodded, not trusting my voice. "I hope so."

"No," Gerald said. "I know so."

—

We kept walking, and I broke the weight with a smirk. "You good, Dad? I should be worried about your health? You sound suspiciously... warm."

He laughed. "Don't get used to it."

But the softness stayed.

Not the words. The **weight** behind them.

—

When Alexis walked in, she didn't try to impress him. Didn't turn it on. She wore jeans, a tucked tee, big gold hoops, and confidence. The kind that didn't need volume.

She walked straight up, offered her hand, and said, "It's good to finally meet you, Mr. Patterson."

Gerald shook her hand and replied, "Please. If you feeding this boy, I owe *you* some respect. Call me Gerald."

They held eye contact a second longer than expected. Then he smiled. A real one. Not just polite.

"You got a good way about you," he said.

Alexis glanced at me, then back at him. "So does your son. He just needed the right rhythm."

He looked at me, then looked away. Not because he didn't agree—but because he did.

—

Later, we sat in my kitchen, just the two of us. Alexis had gone home to prep for an early meeting.

Gerald leaned back in the chair and exhaled.

"She's the one," he said.

"Yeah."

He sipped his tea like it was whiskey.

"Your mama would've liked her."

That hit me.

Because he didn't say it like a compliment.

He said it like he *missed* her again, just from remembering how she loved people.

"She's good to me," I said.

"Don't mess that up," he replied.

"Trying not to."

—

He stood up and walked to the speaker in the corner.

Tapped through my phone's music library until he found what he wanted.

Then he let *"For the Love of You"* ride one more time.

"Play this for her sometime," he said. "But don't say nothin'. Just let it fill the room."

I nodded.

"You gon' propose?" he asked without looking back.

"I'm thinking about it."

"You don't need to think. Just make sure you show up every day after."

Then he turned, and for once—no joke, no jab—just said:

"I like her."

We didn't need more than that.

The song played us out.

And for the first time in my life, I felt like **three people were in the room who believed in me**: the woman I loved, the father who raised me, and the best friend I still talked to in the quiet.

Interlude: Soul Rebels — Reflection Eternal ft. De La Soul

"We don't live for hip-hop / Hip-hop, it lives for us."

—

Rodney was tightening the tech list—double-checking mic levels, sound cues, and which vendors had folding chairs versus actual seating—when Alexis slid beside him with her phone already unlocked.

"I've got an idea."

He smirked. "You always do."

She handed him the screen.

Ms. Metaphor.

Rodney's jaw dropped.

"Wait, *Ms. Metaphor* Ms. Metaphor?"

Alexis nodded once. "Yep."

"She's gonna be here? Like *here* here? That's a real get, Ms. Alexis."

She smiled but didn't say anything right away.

Rodney caught it. "Wait—how'd you even—?"

"That's where it gets better," she said, voice soft now. "Her name's Simone."

Rodney nodded slowly, like the name sounded familiar.

Alexis stepped closer. "Simone Patterson."

He blinked.

Then looked at her like she'd just rearranged the furniture in his mind.

"Pops' daughter?" he said, breath catching on the end of the sentence.

Alexis smiled at the way he said it—*Pops*. Like it had always been true.

Rodney let out a low whistle and shook his head.

"Man. I've been quoting her bars to him for months. He just smiled like he knew good music. He didn't say a word."

"He doesn't have to," Alexis said. "That's the kind of man your father is becoming."

Rodney didn't correct the phrase. He just let it sit.

Alexis tapped the screen again. "She'll do it. No flyer. No name. Just a mic and a moment. For him. For you."

Rodney chuckled, still stunned. "You're wild for this."

"I know," she said. "But admit it—it's kind of perfect."

Rodney stared out over the space they'd built together, his voice softer now.

"I used to wonder what it would feel like to *be* in a crew like the ones we listened to. Tribe. Reflection. Slum. A real family."
He looked over at Alexis. "This feel like that."

She smiled. "Then let's give him something to remember."

Chapter 22: "Lady" — D'Angelo

"I'm tired of hidin' what we feel, I'm tryna come with the real / And I'm gonna make it known, 'cause I want them to know... You're my lady, you're my lady."

—

The Spot had a pulse that night.

Not just music. Not just movement. But a heartbeat—steady, collective, full.

Warm lights poured from inside the building, casting soft glows on brick and chalk murals. Paper lanterns drifted lazily above the courtyard. People gathered around tables, lined up at the food trucks, leaned against walls, held babies, swapped stories.

It was *alive*.

The kind of alive that felt like something had been restored.

—

Rodney was a blur of focus and flow.

Sixteen.
Sixteen, and carrying it all like he'd been doing it for years. Clipboard in hand, hoodie sleeves rolled, headset tugged low over one ear.

He navigated the chaos like a conductor—talking to stagehands, confirming sound cues, checking on vendors, dapping up performers.

I stood off to the side and watched him for a while.
That boy was a rhythm.
A *tempo*.
A walking tribute to Darius's DNA and his own damn will.

And every time I looked at him, I saw flashes—
Me and Darius at that age.
How reckless we were. How alive.
How we never had anything like this.

Rodney did.
And he was *making the most of it*.

—

Dad had settled in the back corner of the courtyard.

Clean. Sharp. The collar of his polo turned down just right under his soft navy blazer. A quiet drink sweating in one hand, the other draped over the back of his chair.

He didn't say much.

Didn't need to.

Every nod, every tap of his fingers on the table, every subtle lean-in said it all.

He was proud.

Not loud. But proud.

I caught him watching Rodney and gave him a quick
look, one that said *"you see that?"*

He didn't nod.
He didn't smile.

He just tipped his chin and raised his glass a half inch.

That was Dad for "damn right I see it."

—

Alexis moved through the space like she was part of
its design.

She was in her lane—graceful, intentional, woven into
the rhythm of the night like an outro that leaves you
full.

Black off-the-shoulder top, jeans, gold hoops.
That's all she needed.

I watched her talk to a couple elders who had just
arrived, guide a young girl to the activity tent, and
stop to smooth the collar of one of the volunteers.
She wasn't hosting the event—*she was anchoring it.*

She found me leaning against the wall near the stage
steps.

"This is love," she said.

I smiled. "You did this."

She gave me a soft look. "No. *They* did this. You just opened the door."

I felt her hand on my chest—just a palm, a small pressure that steadied me. "You feel that?"

"Yeah," I said.

She whispered, "This is what home feels like."

—

Constance sat mid-row on the right side of the courtyard, her palms folded softly in her lap, her smile low and constant. She hadn't said much to anyone— just offered small waves, warm nods, soft greetings.

But her eyes?

They stayed on Rodney.

Watched him cross the stage, manage the mic, make things move.

Her baby.
Her boy.
Her *man*, now.

She blinked slowly, let her gaze follow his footsteps, then closed her eyes for just a moment.

And in that moment, she spoke to Darius like he was sitting right beside her.

"You see him, baby?
He got your eyes, but he got my steadiness.
He don't run. He leads.
I wish you could see him in all this light.
He's doin' right, Darius.
Our boy's doin' right."

A tear slipped down and settled at the edge of her smile.

She wiped it away and sat up straighter.

Because if Darius *was* beside her—spirit or not—he'd want to see her proud, too.

—

Backstage, Simone tightened the mic clip with one hand and let the other rest over her heart.

Her hoodie was zipped halfway. Her braids were tied back. Her journal rested on a nearby stool, pages dog-eared and worn.

She could hear the crowd. The laughter. The breath before applause.

She didn't have her father's eyes on her yet.

That was the point.

He knew she was Ms. Metaphor now—but he didn't know she was here. Didn't know she'd flown in. Didn't know she'd stepped into this room ready to be fully seen—not just as Ms. Metaphor, not just as Simone, but as both.

As all.

And a few rows from the stage, Maya sat quietly.

No fanfare. No announcement. Just presence.

She wore a denim jacket and a simple black dress, her hands folded tightly in her lap.

Simone had invited her. And Maya had come— because real love shows up, even if the words aren't ready yet.

Even if the courage has to be borrowed from the person you love most.

—

I didn't know any of this.

All I knew was that the evening felt like *flow*— unforced, vibrant, aligned.

Rodney stepped to the mic between performances and looked out over the sea of familiar faces.

He adjusted his headset, grinned, and said, "Y'all good?"

The crowd responded with cheers and whistles.

Rodney scanned the room. His voice carried, calm but charged.

"We've had a lot of dope folks up here tonight. But this next one? Different."

He looked at Alexis briefly, then back at the mic.

"She's homegrown. She's movement. She's truth in rhythm."

Rodney stepped aside.

And from stage right—

Simone Patterson walked into the light.

Chapter 23: "Ascension (Don't Ever Wonder)" — Maxwell

"It happened the moment / When you were revealed / 'Cause you were a dream that you should not have been / A fantasy real"

—

I didn't recognize her at first.

Not because she looked different—she didn't. Simone had always been the kind of woman who carried her presence like a quiet revolution. You *felt* her before you understood her.

But tonight, under those lights, standing on that stage with nothing but a mic and her full self?

She wasn't just my daughter.

She was her *own*. Entirely.

—

She didn't look at me right away.

She stood there for a long breath—head down, eyes closed, letting the room settle.

Then she reached for the mic and said, calmly:

"This is for anybody who's ever had to tuck away the loudest parts of themselves just to keep the peace."

You could feel the air change.

The crowd got still.

Simone opened her eyes.

And then she *rhymed*.

—

She didn't come with theatrics. No hypeman. No overworked metaphor.

She just *spoke*—in tempo. In truth.

Verses about growing up with questions no one wanted answers to. About learning silence in a house that echoed. About love that arrived late but landed soft.

She wove in pain. In patience.
Talked about forgiveness as a practice, not a destination.
Talked about her mama's rhythm and her father's record collection.

Talked about being a daughter. A dream. A name she chose herself.
And somewhere in that verse—

I realized she wasn't rhyming to impress.

She was rhyming to be *whole*.

———

It felt like the years were folding in on themselves.

Me holding her as a toddler, one arm around her tiny body while the other reached for diapers I kept forgetting to restock.
Me missing birthday parties when I thought I was chasing something worthwhile.
Me showing up late to a school play and standing in the back, hoping she didn't notice.

She did.
She always did.

And yet here she was. Not just here, but *giving*.

Offering this whole room a version of herself I never got to see in real time.

Until now.

———

I didn't know when the tears started. I just felt Alexis's hand wrap around mine.

She squeezed.

"You okay?" she whispered.

"No," I whispered back. "I'm better."

I looked over at Dad. He wasn't nodding. Just leaning forward slightly. His version of stunned.

Constance had her hand on her heart, her eyes soft and wet.

Rodney's mouth was slightly open, like he couldn't believe what he was seeing. A quiet smile started creeping across his face, like he knew a secret about the world now.

And in the third row, Maya was still. Upright. Holding Simone with her eyes. A kind of *spiritual applause*.

I didn't know who Maya was yet. Not officially.

But when Simone looked her way between lines—and smiled, just barely—
I knew.

———

Simone finished with no big closer.

No tagline. No drop.

She just stepped back from the mic, head bowed slightly. Then she looked out at the crowd. Her eyes found me.

Held me.

I stood.

Not clapping.

Not shouting.

Just *standing*.

And nodding like my father taught me to do.

———

After, I walked around back—cutting through the quiet corners and side doors until I found her near the small prep room, leaning against a table, her palms flat on the wood like she was steadying herself.

She looked up when she saw me.

Didn't move.

Didn't flinch.

"Hey," I said.

"Hey," she replied.

I stood a few feet away, took her in.

"You were…," I started, then stopped. "I don't even have a word for what you just did."

She smiled. "You don't need one."

We stood there for a beat. The music from the stage muffled by the walls.

Then I said, "You good?"

She took a breath.

"I'm better than I've ever been."

I nodded.

And then I stepped closer.

Wrapped my arms around her.

And held my daughter—not like she was fragile, but like she had just come back from the stars.

———

When we let go, she looked past me.

Rodney was standing there, unsure if he should say anything.

Simone walked over, closed the space with calm and confidence, and reached out her hand.

"You did good," she said.

Rodney took it. "You did better."

They held that shake a second longer than needed. Then both nodded.

It was the beginning of something—respect, legacy, maybe even protection.

Big sister. Little brother. No blood needed.

———

As Simone walked back toward the courtyard, I watched her pause by a seat in the third row.

Maya stood.

They didn't kiss. They didn't touch. They just looked at each other like they knew what came next would matter even more.

And then Simone smiled, turned back toward the crowd—

And stepped back into the world like it had always been waiting for her.

Chapter 24: "Nothing Even Matters" — Lauryn Hill ft. D'Angelo

"Now the skies could fall / Not even if my boss should call / The world, it seems so very small / 'Cause nothing even matters at all."

———

The courtyard was winding down, but nobody really wanted to leave.

Some lingered near the food trucks, hugging slow and talking low. Others stood in small circles, dapping up, laughing like they hadn't in years. Even the DJ, who was supposed to be off an hour ago, kept sliding one more record into the mix.

I stood by the stage steps, watching it all—Simone off to the side, talking to Constance and Rodney. Dad in deep conversation with one of the older barbers from the neighborhood. The Spot had never felt more like a home.

Then I felt her beside me.

Alexis.

She didn't say anything at first. Just leaned her head against my shoulder.

We stood there for a while like that.
Not moving.
Not rushing.
Not even pretending to say goodbye to the night.

———

Later, back at my place, I cooked.

Just something simple—eggs, a couple of sweet
potato biscuits we didn't eat earlier, and a few slices
of plantain she'd brought over the week before.

She sat on the counter, legs swinging, hoodie zipped
up over that off-shoulder top. Hair pulled back. Her
skin glowing even in the soft kitchen light.

No music playing.

Just the *hum* of quiet. The kind that only shows up
when you don't need to prove anything.

———

"I'm proud of you," she said.

I looked over from the stove. "For what?"

"For making room for all this."

I turned down the burner.

"You did that too," I said.

She tilted her head. "You ever think about how this started?"

I nodded. "You were playing Juvenile at nine in the morning."

She grinned. "And you were judging me."

"I was confused," I laughed.

She came over to the stove, slid her arms around my waist, rested her head against my back. I turned the burner off. Just stood there with her holding me like that.

"Can I ask you something?" I said.

"You just did," she replied, playful.

"I'm serious."

She stepped back just enough to meet my eyes. "Go on."

"What did you think of me when we first met?"

She raised an eyebrow, surprised and impressed.

"Look at you," she said. "That took some courage."

"Don't dodge the question."

She grinned. "Alright. I thought—'He's got something quiet in him. Like he's walked through a lot. But he ain't hiding.'"

I blinked. "That's a lot to read off a man handing you a volunteer clipboard."

She shrugged. "I've got a gift."

She leaned in again, lips grazing mine. "And I was right."

———

We ate on the couch, legs tangled, plates on our laps. Light conversation. Shoulder touches. Shared looks that said more than the words did.

Afterward, I rinsed the plates and came back to find her curled in the corner of the couch, head resting on her hand, scrolling slowly through pictures on her phone from the event.

She looked up.

"I love your people."

"I love that you're part of them."

She tilted her head. "You ever think... about what's next?"

I paused, then nodded. "All the time."

She waited, like she wanted me to say more.

But I didn't. Not yet.

Because I knew—deep in my chest, in that quiet part of my gut that always warned me and guided me—that the *next* was coming.

And it wasn't something I wanted to do tired. I didn't want to stumble into it.

I wanted to *stand in it.*

———

Later, she drifted off to sleep with her head in my lap while I gently traced circles on her back with my fingertips.

I didn't need to move.

Didn't need to say a word.

Just sat there, eyes closed, heart full, knowing...

Tomorrow was the day.

And everybody I loved would already be in town.

Chapter 25: "Forever My Lady" — Jodeci

"Forever my lady / It's like a dream / I'm holding you close / You're keeping me warm / If this is ecstasy (forever my lady) / Forever my lady / I say just what I mean / Forever and ever / I pray is what I see"

The sun came up slow, like it knew something was about to happen and didn't want to interrupt.

My house was still, save for the rhythm of Alexis's breath against the pillow and the soft creak of the floor under my bare feet.

She was curled on her side, tangled in one of my old t-shirts again—black, soft from too many washes, sleeves a little too long, just the way she liked it. Her arm was bent beneath her head, face completely at peace, as if the night had kissed every worry away.

I stood in the doorway and watched her sleep, a quiet pressure blooming in my chest.

This wasn't about nerves.

It was *readiness*.

I slipped into the kitchen, took the ring from its hiding place inside an old coffee tin, and held it in my palm.

Simple. Timeless. Like her.

I thought about everything that brought us here—Darius, The Spot, Simone, the years that almost swallowed me whole. The days I thought I wasn't capable of this kind of softness. This kind of clarity. This kind of love.

And now?

I didn't just want this life.

I was ready to *build* it. Day by day. Verse by verse. Side by side.

She stirred just after seven, stretching with that subtle hum she didn't even know she made. Her lashes fluttered. Then her eyes met mine.

"Hey," she said, voice still warm with sleep.

"Hey."

She blinked slowly. "Why are you looking at me like that?"

I smiled. "Like what?"

"Like I'm the sunrise."

I sat beside her on the edge of the bed, reached out, tucked a curl behind her ear.

"You are."

She propped herself up on one elbow. "You okay?"

"I'm more than okay."

Then, before I could talk myself out of it, I stood and walked into the next room.

Returned with a folded page from my journal in one hand—and something smaller in the other.

It wasn't dramatic. It wasn't orchestrated.

It was just me, bare feet on hardwood, soul bare in my chest.

I dropped to one knee.

Her eyes widened, and her hand came to her chest before I even said a word.

"Alexis…" I began, steady.

"I don't want to waste good breath. So let me say this right."

"I've loved you in stages. In moments. In silences. In inside jokes and quiet looks across The Spot when nobody else saw me seeing you."

"I've loved you through every beat of becoming the man I never thought I'd get to be."

"You've been my peace and my push. My mirror and my melody."

"And now…"

I opened the small velvet box.

"I want to love you in full."

She covered her mouth. Her eyes shimmered—liquid, full, and wide with joy.

But I wasn't finished.

"I want the mornings. The messy ones. The ones with burnt toast and off-key singing and your earrings on my dresser."

"I want the hard conversations. The real ones. The ones where we choose each other again, even when it's not perfect."

"I want to build something so real with you, it makes the whole world feel like background noise."

I paused.

Then I looked up at her, and said what I came here to say:

"Will you marry me?"

She didn't answer right away.

Instead, she slid off the bed, moved slowly until she was kneeling in front of me, hands cradling my face, her thumb brushing the corner of my eye.

"I've been yours in pieces for a while now," she whispered. "But this... this is all of me."

She smiled through her tears.

"Yes, Malik. In every way. For every season. To infinity and back."

I wrapped my arms around her and held her like the sky might try to take her if I let go.

She buried her face in my neck. I kissed the top of her head.

We stayed like that—knees on hardwood, hearts pressed together, the whole house wrapped in something holy.

Later, we sat on the floor, backs against the bed, her head resting on my shoulder as she turned the ring in the light, studying it like a constellation.

"You sure?" she asked softly.

I kissed her temple.

"I've never been more sure of anything in my life."

The city was starting to wake. The birds were louder. A neighbor's dog barked twice.

But in that moment, wrapped in her, ring glinting, hearts loud but steady—

The only thing that mattered was this:

She said yes.

And forever?

Forever looked just like her.

Epilogue: "Who We Are (Outro)"

"Whenever, wherever, whatever."
—Maxwell

The Spot was still buzzing, even as folks started packing up tables and folding chairs. You could feel it—like the music had soaked into the walls, into the floorboards, into the breath of the building.

No one really wanted to leave.
Not right away.

The benefit had been everything Rodney imagined.
Everything Simone embodied.
Everything *we* needed.

Alexis stood beside me, fingers loosely looped with mine, sipping the last of her iced hibiscus tea. That post-event glow sat on her skin like a halo. I couldn't stop looking at her, which she pretended not to notice until she side-eyed me and whispered:

"Still staring?"

"I'm studying," I said. "Trying to figure out how I pulled this off."

She smirked. "Took you long enough."

Simone had just stepped down from an impromptu mic moment—nothing heavy. Just a few bars off the

top about love and light and roots. Maya stood
nearby, not holding her hand this time, but close
enough that it didn't matter.

I caught Simone's eye. She smiled.

Not a performance smile.
A daughter-sees-her-daddy-seeing-her kind of smile.

And I smiled back.

"You happy?" I asked her later, quietly.

"Yeah, Dad," she said. "Real happy."

"Then that's all I need."

Gerald, Rodney, and I sat off to the side on the low
steps near the mural.
Constance had just handed Rodney a bottle of water
and kissed him on the cheek before slipping inside to
help with cleanup.

Rodney exhaled like he'd been holding his breath all
night.

"You did that," I told him.

He shrugged like he wasn't trying to show how proud
he was of himself.

Then he looked at me, then at my father.

"I wanna be the kind of man Darius was," he said. "But also… the kind you are now."

Gerald's voice came out lower than usual.

"Then you already ahead of both of us."

I stared straight ahead and let that sit.

Then I said, "We make each other better. That's the job."

Rodney nodded, real slow.

Constance found me later while Alexis was helping Simone and Maya load up some equipment. She didn't say much—just stepped beside me, hands tucked into her light jacket, her earrings catching the last bit of the sun.

"Thank you," she said.

"For what?"

"For loving my boy the way Darius would've. You gave him roots, Malik."

I swallowed something thick in my throat.

"He gave me legacy."

We didn't tell everybody right then.

About the engagement.

But Simone already knew. She clocked it from across the room.
Alexis's left hand didn't move like it used to, and her smile had a secret inside it.

She leaned into my side as we watched Simone hug Gerald goodbye. Then Rodney. Then Maya.

"They're really family," she whispered.

"All of 'em," I said.

She turned to me. "We should tell them soon."

"We will," I said. "But for tonight, this is ours."

The Spot emptied slowly, like a good record fading out.
The last to leave were always the real ones—the ones who helped you build it. The ones who knew where the brooms were. The ones who never asked for credit.

Simone stepped back on stage one more time.

No intro. No preamble.

Just the beat of a soul that knew her place.

Her words were soft but strong:

"We not perfect, but we present.
We show up. We stay.
We fight, we build, we raise.

We remember.
We forgive.
We love.
And this—
right here—
is who we are."

And as she stepped down, the lights flickering low, I stood there with Alexis at my side, Gerald leaning just behind me, Rodney snapping a selfie with the mural, Simone slipping into Maya's waiting arms, and Constance humming under her breath as she swept one last corner—

I knew the map was never really about direction.

It was about connection.

The kind that holds you, names you, remakes you.

The kind you choose.

The Legend — Soundtrack Appendix

Each chapter in *The Legend* is named after and inspired by a song that echoes its emotional tone, lyrical rhythm, or narrative turning point. These songs shaped the storytelling, stitched through the lives of Malik, Alexis, Simone, Rodney, and everyone who found themselves in the map.

Prologue

"Prologue"
I Need Love (LL Cool J, 1987)
"I'm alone in my room, sometimes I stare at the wall"

Chapter 1

"Sweet You"
Sweet You (Phonte, 2018)
"Some say it was a blessing in disguise / Scratch that, girl you are a lesson from the skies"

Chapter 2

"Picture Perfect"
Picture Perfect (Eric Roberson, 2014)
"Girl, you are picture perfect"

Chapter 3

"On The Way"
On The Way (Little Brother, 2005)

"Now we on the way y'all, we on the way y'all / The shinin light lookin for a better day y'all"

Chapter 4

"Afro Blue"
Afro Blue (Robert Glasper ft. Erykah Badu, 2012)
"Dream of a land my soul is from"

Chapter 5

"Who Loves You More"
Who Loves You More (Phonte, 2011)
"I tried to change my ways and pray that maybe I can save my life"

Chapter 6

"Prototype"
Prototype (OutKast, 2003)
"I hope that you're the one / If not, you are the prototype"

Chapter 7

"Golden"
Golden (Jill Scott, 2004)
"Living my life like it's golden"

Interlude

"Something in the Way (You Make Me Feel)"
(Stephanie Mills 1989)
"Something in the way you make me feel (Oh, it's something) / Feel (Yes, it's something), feel (I tell you, baby) / Something in the way you make me feel / Feel (Oh), feel (And it makes me feel real good, real good)"

Chapter 8

"For The Cool In You"
For The Cool In You (Babyface, 1993)
"Here we go 'round, and 'round, and 'round, and back, and forth, you know / Everybody goes through it sometime, and that's just the way it flows"

Chapter 9

"Love Is You"
Love Is You (Chrisette Michele, 2007)
"Love is kind when the world is cold / Love stays strong when the fight gets old"

Chapter 10

"Euphorium (Back to the Light)"
Euphorium (Back to the Light) (Phonte, 2018)
"Been feeling real good man, when I see myself / First time in my life feeling like I can finally be myself"

Chapter 11

"Joy and Pain"
Joy and Pain (Maze ft. Frankie Beverly, 1980)
"Joy and pain are like sunshine and rain"

Chapter 12

"Simply Beautiful"
Simply Beautiful (Al Green, 1972)
"If I gave you my love / I'd tell you what I'd do"

Chapter 13

"Whenever You're Around"
Whenever You're Around (Jill Scott, 2007)
"I'm lonely whenever you're around"

Chapter 14

"Love Me Still"
Love Me Still (Chaka Khan, 1995)
"I've wandered far, I've had my fill / I need you now, do you love me still?"

Chapter 15

"Get It Together"
Get It Together (Beastie Boys ft. Q-Tip, 1994)
"Got to get it together and see what's happening"

Chapter 16

"Ms. Metaphor"
Original Chapter Title (N/A, N/A)
"N/A"

Chapter 17

"The Meaning Of The Name"
The Meaning Of The Name (Gang Starr, 1991)
"This is the meaning of the name"

Chapter 18

"Family Business"
Family Business (Kanye West, 2004)
"This is family business / And this is for the family that can't be with us"

Chapter 19

"Good Morning Sunshine"
Good Morning Sunshine (Little Brother, 2019)
"Imagination's not the same as truth / Be careful what your mind could lead into"

Chapter 20

"I Couldn't Love You More"
I Couldn't Love You More (Sade, 1992)
"I couldn't love you more if I tried"

Chapter 21

"For the Love of You"
For the Love of You (The Isley Brothers, 1975)
"Drifting on a memory / Ain't no place I'd rather be than with you"

Interlude

"Soul Rebels"
(Reflection Eternal ft. De La Soul 2000)
"We don't live for Hip-Hop / It lives for us"

Chapter 22

"Lady"
Lady (D'Angelo, 1995)
"You're my lady"

Chapter 23

"Ascension (Don't Ever Wonder)"
Ascension (Don't Ever Wonder) (Maxwell, 1996)
"It happened the moment / When you were revealed"

Chapter 24

"Nothing Even Matters"
Nothing Even Matters (Lauryn Hill ft. D'Angelo, 1998)
"You're part of my identity / I sometimes have the tendency / To look at you religiously"

Chapter 25

"Forever My Lady"
Forever My Lady (Jodeci, 1991)
"Forever my lady / It's like a dream / I'm holding you close / You're keeping me warm"

Epilogue

"Epilogue"
Whenever Wherever Whatever (Maxwell,
1996)
"Whenever, wherever, whatever"

Fair Use and Reference Statement

The Legend draws creative and emotional influence from a collection of iconic songs and artists across Hip-Hop, R&B, and Soul music. Chapter titles and quoted lyrics are used intentionally to reflect the spirit of the story, deepen character arcs, and celebrate the cultural significance of the music that helped shape these voices — both fictional and real.

All referenced lyrics and song titles are the intellectual property of their respective copyright holders. They are used here under the principles of **Fair Use** for the purposes of artistic commentary, transformative storytelling, and homage. No commercial claim is made to the music or lyrics themselves, and no profits are derived from the musical works referenced.

Every effort has been made to properly attribute each song and its creators in the **Soundtrack Appendix** found at the back of this book.

If you're moved by the music featured here, I encourage you to support the artists: stream their albums, buy their records, attend their shows, and share their work.

Acknowledgments

Writing *The Legend* has been a journey of rhythm, memory, and love. To every soul who ever found themselves in a lyric, this one is for you.

Thank you to my family — both by blood and by bond — for teaching me what it means to show up, to grow, and to forgive. Your stories live in me.

To the storytellers of sound — the MCs, the producers, the poets behind the beats — thank you for building the sonic scaffolding that holds this novel up.

Special thanks to those who believed in this story when it was just an idea in a notebook. You know who you are, and I carry your encouragement every time I write.

Kendrick — I will carry your memory forever.

To the readers who see themselves in Malik, Simone, Alexis, or anyone in between — I'm honored you let this book be part of your journey.

About the Author

Perry D. Jones is a storyteller with soul. His writing blends love, legacy, and the echoes of hip hop — always grounded in truth. Whether crafting contemporary character-driven novels or exploring untold Black histories through historical fiction, Perry writes with heart and with purpose.

The Legend is the companion to *The Map*, a novel that introduced readers to Malik Patterson's world of memory, music, and meaning. Perry is also the author of the historical fiction novels *Archer: A Discovered Legacy* and *Dicey: A Legacy of Strength* — two interwoven stories rooted in identity, education, and generational survival.

When not writing, Perry explores family genealogy, studies Black history, and digs for vinyl gems. He is the founder of Synergy Books and believes the best stories are the ones that resonate like your favorite track.

"I'm gonna take the time to drop a dope line." — MC Lyte

Also by Perry D. Jones

• *The Map* — The novel that began Malik Patterson's story. A lyrical, heartfelt exploration of music, grief, and finding your way back to yourself.

• *Archer: A Discovered Legacy* — A historical fiction novel tracing a Black family's journey through education, identity, and endurance.

• *Dicey: A Legacy of Strength* — A powerful companion novel to *Archer*, rooted in Black womanhood, memory, and survival.

Discover more at http://www.synergybooks.co/

Reading Group Questions for *The Legend*

1. How has Malik changed between *The Map* and
    The Legend? What do you think is the most
    meaningful shift in his character?
2. Alexis becomes central to Malik's emotional
    clarity. What does their relationship teach us
    about second chances and soft places to land?
3. How do Simone's secrets — both as an MC
    and in her love life — mirror her father's own
    journey of identity and authenticity?
4. Rodney becomes more than a reminder of
    Darius — he becomes family. How did that
    transition unfold for you as a reader?
5. Gerald's evolution is quiet but impactful.
    What did you make of his late-in-life
    openness? How did it affect your
    understanding of Malik?
6. The benefit event becomes a beautiful
    convergence. What does it say about legacy,
    art, and community as healing spaces?
7. Ms. Metaphor is Simone's alter ego — and a
    metaphor in itself. What did her music
    symbolize for the Patterson family story?
8. What was your reaction to the proposal
    scene? Did you feel like it was earned?
9. Constance and Alexis are very different
    women, but both shape Malik's life in major
    ways. How do you think he grows from
    knowing them?
10. Music still anchors the narrative. Which song
    chapters hit you the hardest, and why?

11. How does the story redefine what "family" looks like?

12. If *The Map* was about finding direction, what does *The Legend* become? What kind of "legend" did Malik ultimately create?